The Princess and the Snowbird

Also by Mette Ivie Harrison

The Princess and the Hound
The Princess and the Bear

The Princess and the Snowbird

METTE IVIE HARRISON

An Imprint of HarperCollinsPublishers

HarperTeen is an imprint of HarperCollins Publishers.

Library of Congress Cataloging-in-Publication Data is available.
ISBN 978-0-06-155317-2

Typography by Hilary Zarycky
10 11 12 13 14 CG/RRDB 10 9 8 7 6 5 4 3 2 1
❖
First Edition

For my mother

PROLOGUE

The Tale of the Snowbirds

THOUSANDS OF YEARS ago, before humans ruled the world, the snowbirds flew above the earth and watched over the flow of the first, pure aur-magic, spreading the power to all, and making sure that every creature had a share. The name *snowbird* came, some say, because their nesting grounds were in the northern mountain isles, where the snow never melted. Others say they were named for their appearance, for these creatures with huge wingspans seemed pure white except when the sun rose from behind and showed the silver threaded through their feathers.

Like all other creatures, snowbirds had to kill to live, but they were wise and swift and never gave pain to those who died for them. And when a snowbird died, no ounce of its aur-magic was lost. The magic flowed out of it back into the wild, for use by all the living.

But as humans learned magic, the snowbirds began

to disappear. One by one, then dozens at a time. The more the humans spread over the world, the more the snowbirds had to pass out of it. Even the snowbirds who survived laid fewer eggs.

But snowbirds were not the only creatures affected by human use of magic. The moose shrank in size until their antlers were no longer as large as the snowbird's wingspan. Wolves became tame enough to live in groups rather than as solitary individuals. And some species disappeared entirely.

When no new snowbird chicks had hatched for a hundred years, the leader of the snowbirds, Tulo the Hopeless, called a meeting with all his kind. There were now only six snowbirds remaining—too few to fly together and still keep watch over the land and its creatures—so Tulo assigned each snowbird a region to watch over and heal. It was the only way Tulo could think of to continue to fulfill the snowbirds' mission, but he was afraid that this was the end, of both the aur-magic and the snowbirds. Soaring alone above the mountains, he feared that he might never again see his own kind.

As the years passed, Tulo felt the death cries of the remaining snowbirds one by one. The first, Frest the Fierce, died after he had poured out waves of magic trying to cure the land nearest the humans, but to no avail. Tulo arrived too late to save Frest, and as he passed over the land, he could sense how it had lost its wildness. It could no longer absorb Tulo's aur-magic, and he could do nothing to change that.

The next to die was Rikiki the Swift, for she had gone too far south into human lands and had no strength to return. Her call was faint, a final farewell.

Then Stowr died, without a sound. Tulo never found a trace of the snowbird who had been a childhood friend and with whom he had molted first feathers.

Uvi died on the ground, mauled by the very animal she had tried to offer aur-magic to. The wolf had learned deceit and lust for power from humans and did what wolves would never have done before this time. It called for its pack while the snowbird was most vulnerable, weak and with her wings tucked to herself to keep warm. The pack cut her head and body to pieces, but the wings were left untouched, bits of aur-magic still clinging to them, untaken. When Tulo swooped down, he took the magic to himself, because it was what must be done.

The last was Wara, the youngest of the snowbirds. Tulo had watched over her when she was a chick, and had thought her strong and beautiful. He called to her each time another died, and each time she asked whether she should come to him so that they could mourn together, as the snowbirds had once done. Each time he refused, for he could not see how mourning would change death. And there was still land to be protected with aur-magic against the humans who seemed to take it for their own use and never replenish it.

Then the day came when Wara herself called out in

pain to Tulo, and he rushed to her. She had been struck in the wing by a human arrow as she flew above a newly built village. She tried to fly on, but part of her wing had gone numb. When Tulo reached her, she was clinging to the edge of a cliff, the wind whistling around her in a furor.

Tulo swooped down and pulled her away from the edge. He immediately felt the loss of magic in Wara's wing. The magic bled out of her, but Tulo could not take it back to himself. It had changed into something tainted by humans, something magic and yet not aur-magic. It was a terrible thing. Tulo did not know how he could help Wara, but he determined at least he would not leave her to die alone.

Tulo tucked his own wings close and gentled Wara with soft words, sung with the melody of the sun and the harmony of the moon. Wara leaned her neck into his. Tulo breathed in her smell, surprised at how much he had missed being with other snowbirds.

But he hated the arrow in her and began to tug at it with his beak.

"Yes, take it out. I will die bleeding freely," Wara sang back to him, and Tulo admired her courage, though her voice was thready with pain and still high-pitched with youth.

Tulo worked at the arrow until he had pulled it out of her flesh entirely.

She sagged to the ground and took in great, gasping breaths of air.

4

When she had fallen asleep, and was breathing calmly once more, Tulo examined the arrowhead more carefully. The tip was made from a strange stone, light-colored and brittle, with a cold scent. Tulo did not dare touch it directly, for fear it would numb him as well. But when he closed his eyes and looked only with his magic, he saw that the stone cut two ways, into the flesh and into the aur-magic. The flesh might heal, but the aur-magic had bled away and could not be returned.

While Wara slept, Tulo held the shaft of the arrow in his beak and flew far out over the ocean. He flew until he had reached the iciest part of the world, where no animals lived and even the creatures of the sea kept away. There, at last, he flung the evil weapon down until he heard it shatter on the tip of an iceberg. He then returned to Wara to ease her pain. He could do nothing for the one wing, but he could offer her food and drink, and himself. She rested and sang about the future with her fine voice, though so much had changed.

After many days, Wara recovered enough that Tulo believed she would not die. He coaxed her into trying her first flight without the full use of her wing. She was shaky and lopsided, and Tulo had to fly beneath her to keep her in the air. He dared not try for the nesting grounds, not yet, but they flew away from the humans as far to the north as they could.

Each day they struggled to go farther, to eat, to keep safe from humans. And each day, Tulo fell more in love with the snowbird whom he had once thought of as a chick. In turn, Wara fell in love with the old snowbird she had once thought angry and wretched. They were the last of their kind, and they expected to die together.

But one morning Wara woke and felt the strains of birth upon her. Tulo had already left in the dark cold of morning to go hunting. Alone, Wara squatted and pressed the egg out of her body. She nudged it with her beak and tried to sense the magic in it, but it was not until Tulo came home that she was sure, for he, too, sensed the great aur-magic within the egg.

"More aur-magic than in either of us. More aur-magic than any snowbird has ever had." He spoke aloud what neither could fully believe, yet both felt.

"What does it mean?" asked Wara.

Day by day, the two waited. Tulo went for food when he must, but both worked to keep the egg warm.

At last the egg cracked open and the small snowbird emerged.

"What shall we call him?" asked Wara.

"Tululare," said Tulo, for it meant "the last call of hope."

This was the story told and retold by those who loved the old aur-magic and hated the new tehr-magic that humans used to abuse the world. From mother to son, father to daughter, grandparent to grandchild the story went, in hope that one day there would be a cleansing of the magic and that the new would return to old.

BOOK ONE
Liva and Jens

CHAPTER ONE

Liva

*L*IVA DID NOT think of her age in years, for that
was a human habit. She did not even think of
her age in seasons, because she did not bother
to count them—only humans counted. Liva equally
enjoyed the bright sky of summer; the wet, verdant green
of spring; the colors of autumn; and the darker sky of
winter. She did not long for one while she had the other.
Each season was its own. There were animals who lived
through only one season, and those who lived through
many, as she did.

One day Liva sat in her cave, practicing birdcalls
as she changed from one form to the next: plover, eider,
crake, dovekie, grebe, and dipper. She enjoyed the sensation of one form sliding into the next, and each time
she went through the repetition, she sped it up. She was
caught in the midst of a transformation when she heard
the sound of ragged breathing at the mouth of the cave.

Her mother limped toward her, trailing blood, her hind leg torn so that it hung the wrong way.

"Mother!" Liva called out, taking her mother's shape, the shape of a wild hound, rare in the north. She lunged forward and licked at her mother's wound, but it was too deep to staunch with only her saliva.

"What happened?" Liva asked in the language of the hounds, for it was the only language her mother could now speak, since she had given the great gift of her aur-magic to Liva at birth.

"A white wolf," gasped the hound. "Starving. I should have avoided him. But I have my pride."

"I will kill him," Liva threatened. She leaned forward and sniffed her mother's flank, to get a sense of the white wolf. She was excellent at tracking, and she was certain she would find the wolf not long after she left the cave. If he was hungry, he would make mistakes, and though she was not full grown, she could defeat him.

"No, Liva," said her mother. And then she bit out a cry of pain.

Liva stared at her, frightened. She had never seen her mother unable to control herself this way. "I will!" Liva said. "You cannot stop me. I will do what I want."

"Please," her mother whispered, her head low to the ground, though she did not allow herself to fall to her side. "Stay with me, Liva. I need you with me now."

Liva sighed and put her head under her mother's. "I will go for Father, then," she said. "He will kill the wolf instead, and then he will come and make you well again."

She said this though her father had also given up his aur-magic to his daughter. He had only enough magic to remain a bear, though he had been born a man. In the forest a bear and a hound could protect a child better than humans could, for a hound was fast and had an acute sense of smell, while a bear was very large and had a roar loud enough to shake the river from its banks.

"No," her mother said again. "He is too far away for you to go to him. And he has more important things to do. There are lives that depend on him."

"Your life depends on him," whimpered Liva. She did not like to show her fear. An animal that showed its fear was weak. That was the law of the forest that Liva had learned since she had first begun to take animal shapes as a small child.

"Those with aur-magic in the south are hunted down and if captured put to death. Your father must help them stay free. But I will recover," said her mother. "All I need is time. And you." She nuzzled Liva.

It distracted Liva for a little while. Then her mother quieted and closed her eyes. Her breathing was still sharp and uneven, but Liva thought the hound was asleep.

Liva examined the wound with her eyes, with her nose, and then with her magic. The leg was damaged beyond repair. There were veins that had been cut off, scar tissue forming around muscles that would stiffen them.

11

Ever since Liva could remember, her mother had refused to take Liva's magic to shape herself into an animal for play. Liva did not understand why. She had plenty of aur-magic for them both.

Now Liva put a paw to her mother's leg. The hound winced and tensed up the leg. In that moment, Liva pressed magic into the wound.

But the magic rebounded to her painfully, thrust back by her mother. "Liva, leave it be," said the hound, opening her eyes for just a moment, as if she were too tired to do so for long.

Liva was confused. "I can fix your wound," she said. "I can. I can see how to do it." Could she be afraid that Liva would damage her leg?

"I do not doubt it," said her mother. "But you must not use your magic on me."

"It is not just for play," Liva insisted.

"No, but I've had my chance with the aur-magic already." The hound's words were slurred, and it seemed to Liva as though she was only partly herself. Surely that must be why she was not making any sense.

"Just a little," said Liva, persisting. Her father had tried that on her, when she was ill, and he wanted her to take in some broth. She had taken a single sip, just to stop the noise of his pleading. But then she had found that it tasted wonderful, that the warmth that struck her stomach was just what she could have wished for, so she had taken more and more.

"None," said her mother, growling at her.

So Liva left the cave. She hunted for dinner, and brought back some of the carcass for her mother. Her mother would not touch the meat. She was too weak, and turned to her other side, sleeping heavily. The hound would not stir even when Liva tried to wake her to move closer to the far side of the cave.

Instead Liva pulled the furs over from the far side of the cave. She draped them around her mother's shoulders, changing into human form briefly because human hands were the most useful for this task.

Then she changed back into a hound and cuddled close to her mother, her back to her mother's front. She fell asleep for a time that way, until she was woken in the middle of the night by the sound of her mother's weeping.

The hound was not awake, but she was weeping in pain, tears streaming down her cheeks and into the dark fur around her neck. Liva went out and got water, filling her mouth with it and then returning to put it into her mother's mouth. After several trips, her mother even swallowed a few of the berries that Liva gathered. The berries her father liked to eat.

Liva thought of her father urgently. He had been gone two months now. Liva hoped that he would return soon. Surely there could not be enough humans with the aur-magic in the south to keep him away longer. The humans she could sense in the village a few hours to the south of the cave, for example, had no aur-magic at all, only the tehr-magic they used to enslave animals and carve into the natural shape of the land.

The next morning Liva realized that her mother was getting worse. Her wounded leg had become inflamed and filled with pus, and the hound either thrashed with fever or was so still that Liva had to put a paw out to see whether she yet breathed. And still, she would not take any magic.

Again Liva considered going out to find her father, though that would mean leaving her mother alone. She did not know what to do. She was out hunting the next day when her father appeared at the river's edge.

"Oh, Father," she wailed in the language of bears. She told him what had happened, weeping.

Her father lifted her to his shoulder.

Liva spoke as clearly as she could. "You must make her take the aur-magic. If I give it to you first, then she will take it. It will not taste like me." Liva tried to send her magic into her father, for surely he would be sensible.

But she instantly sensed him pushing it away fiercely as he put her down. "No magic," he said. "Not from you."

He went back to the cave at a loping run, and there Liva watched as he pressed his mouth to the hound's in a moment of greeting and love. The hound opened her eyes for just a moment and gave him a small smile. Then the bear lifted her awkwardly to his chest and carried her to

14

the bed of pine needles in the back of the cave. Over the next several days, he petted the hound when she shivered, and soothed her when she cried out in pain.

Her mother's fever came down slowly and then the wound on her leg healed, after a fashion. She did not let Liva help it along, not once, no matter how frustrated Liva was at the slow recovery that dragged into winter.

Liva was certain the limp would be permanent. "You should have taken my magic," she said bitterly one day, after her mother let Liva go ahead for the kill in their hunt. "You needed it."

"Yes, but others will need your aur-magic more," said her mother.

"Others—who?" asked Liva.

"You will know when the time has come. Humans have learned to take the aur-magic and never return it. They twist it to their own use and corrupt it entirely. In doing so, they are destroying the wild world. If you are to stop them, you will need every bit of the aur-magic you can gather to yourself. If I took any portion of it, how could I live knowing that it might be my selfishness that hastened the end of the aur-magic?"

But Liva did not care about such larger concerns. She cared about her mother, and about this moment.

So she changed into the shape of a wolf like the one that had attacked her mother and tried to frighten her mother by nipping at her newly healed wounds.

Her mother did not try to stop her but only looked at

her with a steady gaze. "I will be with you as long as I can. I will remember that your magic has a purpose, until you can remember it for yourself."

"If you could not stop the humans from taking the magic for themselves and ruining it, then how will I do it?" asked Liva plaintively.

"Ah, you are stronger than you know, little one," said her mother.

Not strong enough to make her mother take her magic, however. And what use was it then?

Chapter Two

Jens

"COME NOW, COME now," Jens's father said to the black-faced ram. He walked from the gate across the muddy ground to where the animal stood. He put out his hand and moved slowly, crouching so that he seemed shorter than he was, less threatening.

The other sheep stepped away from the one who had been chosen to die.

The ram trembled.

Then Jens saw its head rise. The ram looked his father in the eyes and went still. Jens could not even see the beat of blood in its neck. Its eyes had turned to glass, like in the heads displayed atop spears at the winter feasts.

"Just a bit of cold," his father whispered. He took out his stone knife, different from the knives of the other men in the village, cruder in shape, though just as sharp. The tip of it was white and it was so brittle that it had grown smaller over the years, until Jens did not understand why his father did not replace it, but instead claimed that this knife was better than any other.

His father took a breath and twisted the knife under the ram's neck.

Blood ran out between his father's fingers. There was no struggle.

His father let go of the animal, slipping his knife out of it, and Jens sighed in relief as the carcass fell to the ground.

"Good meat," said his father, leaning over the upturned abdomen. He nodded to himself, then smoothed his hands up and down the skin until he found the right spot to open the carcass.

"Careful not to ruin the skin," his father said, glancing up at Jens. "Worth less, can't make a full coat of it."

Jens's own coat was patched together from two pieces, and he knew what his father meant. Whenever there was wind, Jens felt it pierce him at the small of his back, where the coat was stitched.

"Best knife I ever found. Some of the others in the village say it's an uncanny thing, but it's mine and I've never had an animal move after the blade touched it." He held up the knife to the sun, where it glinted with specks of gray.

"You have to get them close enough with a word they understand, but the knife does the rest." With a few more flicks of the blade, the ram's skin was freed from its flesh.

Jens reached for the skin, but he did not move quickly enough. It fell to the ground.

"Blind, dumb, and deaf!" his father shouted at him. "Useless, since the day you were born. Not a bit of tehr-magic in you. Not a hint of it, that I've ever seen. Might as well give you to the Hunter. He's the only man I've heard of who makes having no magic a virtue."

Jens shivered. The Hunter, who lived in the great port town of Tamberg-on-the-Coast, was ruthless and cruel, and he did not hunt animals. He hunted humans who had the old aur-magic. It was said he had a knife that could cut the aur-magic out through the heart, and when parents were angry, they sometimes warned their children that the Hunter would come for them and take their magic.

It seemed worse still to Jens that his father thought he would go to the Hunter and become like him.

"I am glad your mother is dead, for she would hate to see what you have become. You are nothing like her. Nothing at all."

Jens's mother had died at his birth, and his father had never forgiven him for it.

"Sorry, Father," said Jens, trying to clean off the skin. He seemed only to make it worse.

"Take the knife." His father held it out.

Jens took it, shuddering, though the knife itself felt no different to him than any other.

"Be careful with it," his father said, and held up one

arm to show a livid scar. He always said he had no feeling left in that arm. He would not even flinch when he held it to the fire, which had given him a reputation as both brave and coldhearted.

"Quickly, now. I want to be done with this soon," his father said, rubbing his hands together. "Call it."

Jens opened his mouth, but did not know what to fill it with. He had never been one to talk to animals. He listened to them well enough, but only because the sound was soothing, not because it had any meaning.

"The one with the lame leg," his father directed him. It had been the smallest of the lambs born in the spring, but it had the most beautiful white coat, so clear and pure that it seemed to shine even in the dullest light. It would bring good coin for the hard winter months.

"Come now," said his father.

"Come now," echoed Jens, his voice as wobbly as the lamb's legs.

"No. Not like that. Speak to its heart. Speak as it speaks."

Jens licked his lips. He made a few baaing sounds. Was that what his father meant? He put his hand out, and the lamb kicked up its legs.

"Must I always do your work for you?" His father did—something. He looked at the lamb intensely; it was as though he *thought* at it. Jens knew that his father was using the tehr-magic, but he couldn't sense it himself. What did it feel like? Jens would never know.

The lamb went silent, its eyes on Jens's father.

"Let the knife take its life, and the cutting will be easy," his father promised.

Jens raised the knife, then put it to the lamb's neck. But the lamb twisted away from him and he panicked, letting go of the knife. It fell onto a stone, and the blade shattered.

"Useless!" his father shouted, shoving him back.

Jens knew he deserved it. The stone knife could not be replaced . . . but there was a part of him that was not sorry it was gone.

Taking out a metal knife, his father called to the lamb, which was twitching and crying out in pain, though the stone blade had only cut it lightly on one side.

The metal knife went in deep and clean, and the lamb was finished. It shivered once, then died.

Jens stared at the delicate shards of the stone blade. He kicked dirt at them to cover them up.

His father cursed at him as he sliced open the carcass, then ungloved the flesh, but cut the skin badly. "Blind, deaf, and dumb. Useless. A dead son would be a better one."

CHAPTER THREE

Liva

AFTER HER MOTHER'S injury, Liva noticed the passing of seasons far more. In winter her mother did not leave the cave, as if she were hibernating with the bear. In spring the bear took Liva to gather berries, and when they returned, the hound had done nothing but stare at buds unfurling on the oak tree with the broken limb. In summer, she remained at the edge of the cave for most of the day, or sometimes limped to the stream to get her own water, slipping her whole head in for long stretches of time. In autumn the bear told Liva stories about the ancient aur-magic, and the hound flinched at the sound of the rain and wind, howling through the craggy rocks on the mountains above.

When eight seasons had passed after her mother's injury, the bear began to leave again more frequently, on his rescue missions to the south. He did not tell Liva of them, but she could tell when he had spent the night without sleep after a dream in which he had seen humans with aur-magic in danger. Liva did not understand why so many humans hated the natural aur-magic, though they used the corrupted tehr-magic freely enough. She had tried once to ask her father, and he had only said that humans did not understand what was best for them, and they likely never would.

While her mother spent more time in the cave, Liva spent more time outside in the forest. Liva hated being inactive, and she had been hoping for a while now to find an animal to be her companion.

Liva could take any form, but that did not mean the animals would accept her. Her best hope seemed a young one who would become used to her, but she had tried several times before without success.

Once she had tried to bond with a bear cub, but she had smelled too much of her father, a different bear, and the cub fought with her over and over until she gave up believing it was all in fun.

A second time, she had tried to befriend a nest of baby robins, but they had grown up so quickly and were soon flying away without her. They didn't want her following them, for they were looking to the future and to making their own nests.

Finally she had tried to join with an animal already full grown, a vixen. They had hunted together, and Liva had given up the prey to her friend to prove her trustworthiness. But only a few days later the vixen was ready to mate, and if Liva came too close, she growled and snapped at her. Liva tried again when the vixen was alone, but she was fractious and ill-tempered because of the weight of her pregnancy.

Now Liva was desperate, and she set her sights on a felfrass kit.

Liva had watched the felfrass's birth only a few weeks before: a sleek, black thing with tiny claws, large black eyes, and a face circled in white. A full-grown felfrass was the size of a wild hound, but with the fierceness of a bear and the courage to try to take prey from one if it could. The small felfrass was more the size of a rabbit and twitched like a bunny when Liva was nearby, looking as if it recognized her.

But this was the first day she had tried to approach the kit. She wore the form of a young felfrass herself, following it patiently step by cautious step, focused on nothing else but the kit. It was old enough now to be without its mother. Liva waited until the kit had eaten leisurely by the stream. Then it lay on its back on a warm rock, staring up at the patches of sky visible beneath the canopy of trees. Liva came closer, snuffling, making a few sounds so that her appearance would be no surprise. She spoke a few words in the language of the felfrass about the brightness of the day, the smell of the air after feeding, and the beckoning of the stream.

The felfrass kit poked its head up.

She spoke to it of dancing on rocks and swimming as fish.

The felfrass kit switched its tail in invitation.

It liked her. Surely this was the moment when she had found a creature that understood life in the forest, the freedom and the joy of it, and also the thrill of danger. A felfrass was just arrogant enough not to care that Liva smelled of bear and hound from the cave.

She was reaching out a paw to touch it, to begin a play fight, when suddenly there was a terrible rumbling sound in the forest. Liva looked up to see a whole hunting party of humans, more than a dozen of them, all holding weapons of various kinds.

They wore heavy coats of animal fur pulled up around their faces, as if they thought this would disguise their piercing, human eyes; the smoky, sour smell that hung over them like a cloud; and the scratching sound of their voices in the soft forest air.

Liva remembered from her father's stories that humans were wily and dangerous, unpredictable. And they killed sometimes for pleasure rather than for the need for meat. Certainly when Liva looked into these eyes, they seemed hungry for something that mere flesh would not provide. Her instinct was to run away from them, but a stronger feeling told her to stay. She had to protect her felfrass.

The felfrass was frozen in curiosity, but Liva hid behind a tree. She watched through branches for a few precious moments to see which of the humans were most vulnerable.

Two were smaller than the rest. One was a head shorter than the others, but there was a hard look in his eyes that Liva did not like. The other human was not as small, but he looked more unsure of himself. If she meant to attack the weakest human, he would be the one.

Liva had killed many times in her life, nor did she know of any reason to be ashamed of it. She chose animals that would have died more painfully otherwise, lingering with age or infirmity, and she ate the animal whole when she did kill it, leaving nothing behind but the bones.

The small, uncertain human had no fur around his face, but showed white-blond hair, and he shivered with the cold. His boots were far too big for him, and his hands were bare underneath the long sleeves of the coat. To Liva he looked as innocent as a newborn eaglet—but a newborn eaglet took only a few days before its beak was capable of ripping apart flesh and its claws were good for stabbing directly at the heart.

Liva changed into the form of a wolf, leaping from behind her hiding place and lunging at him with teeth bared. She landed two paws on his chest and threw him backward onto the forest floor. None of the other humans noticed his plight—they were too busy closing in on the kit.

Liva had to make this human cry out first for the help

of the others. They must turn back to him and abandon the felfrass.

The human scrambled to his feet again. When Liva raked a claw across his upper thigh, he turned to her with his hands flapping as a bird's wings in her face, with no hope of actually harming her. The sharpness of his movements caught her eye.

No human face could look handsome to Liva, who was so used to animals. But he had character, and there was a spark of fire in him that Liva liked. Yet when Liva searched for a taste of his magic, she found that he had none at all, neither the aur-magic that was her own nor even the tehr-magic that was so common among humans.

Hesitating at this revelation, Liva was surprised when the small human threw himself at her. Suddenly they were tumbling end over end down a small hillock, toward the stream nearby. She could smell the water.

The human had a hand to her throat. Liva's claws were on his chest, and there was blood streaming down into the top of his trousers. Clearly this human had been hurt before, and instead of giving up, had decided to live. The human looked her in the eyes then.

And stopped.

Liva did not know why he did it. But she did the same. She recognized something in him that was like herself.

It made no sense.

He lived in a village, with other humans.

She lived in the forest, with other animals.

He had no magic of any kind.

She had the wild aur-magic in great plenty.

He was pale and white haired.

She, in her human form, was dark.

But she let go of him, and he took his hand from her throat and got to his feet.

He pointed at her and stepped back. He, too, stared at her as if he were staring at a reflection of himself in a mossy pond, dimly recognizable.

Liva did not know how, but despite her form, he could see in her eyes the truth of what she was.

He knew she was human.

Liva found herself changing. She was smaller than he was in human form and shivering, for she had on no clothing. She had never bothered with it, because she had never changed into human form away from home before.

That was one of the rules her mother had drilled into her since she was born. She could change whenever she wished, into any form she chose, so long as she did not change while humans were watching. They were not to be trusted. They would kill her, her mother had said. No matter what the cost to themselves, they would chase her down. They would kill her and her mother and her father, and her great aur-magic would all be gone—for great aur-magic was what humans feared most of all.

The boy swallowed hard, his eyes wide. He pointed to himself. "Jens," he said. He waited.

"Liva," Liva said at last, her throat dry.

He smiled at her.

Then there was a shrieking cry, of death and despair. Liva knew the sound well. She had heard many animals make it before. Sometimes she had caused them to make it herself, for not all animals welcomed death, even when she warned them of it, or tried to stun them with her magic, to make it easy for them to die.

It was the felfrass.

Liva was angry that she had forgotten about the kit who was her only hope for companionship. A human had made her forget.

She spat at him, then changed herself back into the form of a felfrass, and crashed through the bush to get to the kit.

She reached the circle of humans with their weapons out. The kit was mewling.

Liva growled, a warning to the kit to get away, to flee. But it was not fast enough.

So Liva watched as the kit had its throat cut before her eyes, and she wept with felfrass tears though it was a human thing to do.

Then she gave up a howl and turned her back, running into the forest to the north, back to her cave. When she reached home, she tucked her tail around herself and listened to the quick breathing of her lungs and the beat of her heart.

I am a felfrass.

I am an animal.

I am not human, she thought.

I am not like them!

I am not like him!

I have aur-magic, and I belong in the forest.

I will never leave this place.

But when her mother came to lick her awake the next morning, she was in human form, wrapped in the fur of animals left in the cave. And she could not get the image of the small, uncertain human out of her mind, his eyes staring into hers as if he saw himself for the first time.

CHAPTER FOUR

Jens

JENS WAS SO distracted by thoughts of a girl who had also been a wolf and a felfrass that he did not notice the spring snow fall until he stumbled and fell forward onto his hands and face. He looked around to find the others in the hunting party, but they were nowhere to be seen. He had gotten lost, which was not like him at all. He hated to put himself into a situation where others might laugh at him or have any additional reasons to single him out. He usually did all that he could to make himself unnoticed. How they would mock him when he got back to the village! It was almost enough to make him think about not returning.

But what would he do here? He could not survive alone.

He looked around to check whether there was anything familiar, and that was when he glimpsed it. He had never seen anything like it before. It was magnificent and

31

terrifying, both at once, and he walked slowly toward it.

Standing in the muddy snow of spring, the bird spread out its glistening wings—clean and pure and white and shining with hints of silver, spread out as wide as three men together. *A snowbird,* Jens thought. For he almost thought that it was made of snow, perfectly carved.

The snowbird folded its wings and stared at Jens with black, shiny eyes. As Jens approached, he could see its heart beating rapidly in its breast. Its head alone was bigger than any man Jens had ever seen. He caught his breath at the beauty and sheer size of the snowbird, then put out a hand to steady himself, touching the bird heavily, though it did not flinch.

Was it wounded? He was surprised that it did not fly away from him.

Jens could see the snowbird swallow and its eyes blink. He touched its huge beak, as big as his own leg, and then dared to step to the side and run a finger along its wing.

The snowbird shivered at his touch, so he pulled away. But he could not stop staring. Nor could the snowbird.

"What do you need?" Jens asked. "How can I help you?"

The bird did not startle at his voice but kept to its feet steadily. In its presence, Jens felt the whole world seem different, as if his life in the village, with all its bitterness, was swept away clean. Dazed, he felt he could stay here forever and never think of any need but that of being next to the snowbird. He felt safe and secure, at home as he had never felt anywhere else.

Suddenly the snowbird leaped into the air. Jens put up a hand to call it back, but was stopped at the realization of what the snowbird had left behind. Where there had been just the first hint of spring was now the green glory of summer. Wherever the snowbird had touched the forest floor, flowers bloomed; trees unfurled their leaves so that they were clothed in green; there were butterflies flying around him in bright colors of yellow and blue, bees humming around a beehive that smelled of sweet honey.

Jens stumbled forward, past dark, until he heard at last the voices of the hunting party. He was sure that they mocked him, but he did not hear any of the words. They could not hurt him. Though he had missed his chance this year to prove himself a man in the hunt, he would not have traded meeting the wolf-girl or the snowbird for anything. But he had to be careful to give no hint of what he had seen, for he knew that if they believed him, all of them would be quick to hunt the snowbird for the value of its feathers. As for the wolf-girl—they would search for her until they found her and killed her, for she must have the forbidden aur-magic to transform herself into an animal.

It was not until he had reached the outskirts of the village that Jens realized a huge white and silver feather had been tucked behind his neck. He pulled it out, and felt a sudden constriction in his throat, as though he had swallowed a fish whole.

He put the feather to his face and let it fall gently across his nose. Then he tucked it in the pouch at his side, to be looked at only in private, to remind him of a girl and a magic that could bring summer.

CHAPTER FIVE
Liva

A FTER HER ENCOUNTER with the humans, Liva kept closer to home. She had not fully believed that humans were dangerous before, but now she did. And when he returned, her father seemed to feel the same fear, for he did not leave them for nearly four seasons. Liva told herself that perhaps he was finished leaving them now, that he had grown too old to save undeserving humans.

Though the bear complained about his age, and the cold, and Liva's vicious competitive streak, he raced with her in bear form and played hide-and-seek in the vastness of the forest, which took both time and a good nose. Then, when he was tired, he played language games with her that forced her to use the languages of all the animals she knew. If it was close to bedtime, he would tell her stories of his childhood beginning with "Once, when the magic was younger . . ."

Liva paid rapt attention to every detail, though she was not always sure her father's stories were absolutely true. When he claimed that he had put a bean in his ear and let it grow for two years, and it had to be pulled out by a dozen master woodsmen, all in a row, who fell over onto their backs when at last the great bean tree was pulled free of its roots in his bowels, her mother made dubious sounds.

Some of his stories seemed too young for her, but she listened anyway. Some were meant to teach her lessons. When she bragged about how fast she could run, he told the story of the fish who learned to dance skimming on top of the water and boasted to the others of his kind until he was scooped into a net and carried away to feed a young farmer and his wife.

"I don't dance," said Liva.

"Of course not," said her father.

And he told her the next day the story of a little girl who would not go to bed at night when her mother called for her, and so became lost in the woods and was sadly devoured by a monster of the darkness.

"I am not a little girl, Father," Liva growled at him. "And I know that there are no monsters."

"Just because you have not met any does not mean they do not exist," he replied with a wry bear smile. "Who knows what you might discover when you leave this forest and make a life for yourself away from your mother and me."

It was difficult for Liva to think about leaving her parents and the forest. She did not want to leave, and yet she did not want to be a child in their eyes forever.

"I think I have aur-magic enough to go wherever I please," said Liva with a touch of bravado.

Her mother made a low sound of disapproval, and her father's expression turned grim. He father looked at Liva sternly, and shook a paw at her. "You underestimate the power of humans. You are only one, and they are many, with or without the aur-magic."

Liva thought of the hunting party of humans she had met before. She had not told her parents about them because she thought they would overreact and perhaps forbid her to return to that part of the forest. "But they have no claws, no fur. They cannot run on four legs. They do not even know how to smell their way through the world."

"Even so," said her father. "They are more fierce than a bear and more bloodthirsty than a mountain cat. Keep away from them if you can, Liva. Promise me that."

"I will, Father," said Liva. And she meant it at the time. She was not even interested in humans, except per-haps for that one. And what chance was there that she would ever meet him again?

Then her father was tired and had to rest. After his nap, his stomach rumbled, but he made no move to find food for himself. So Liva dug with her claws to bring him his roots from the river, which was south of the cave, that evening, and the next and the next. She used her teeth to make sure that the beetles were cleaned out from his fur each morning, before they began to bore into his skin. In the following months, as she grew to near full bear height, he began to depend upon her more and more for help, and Liva began to depend upon her own knowledge of the world. Her father might once have known more of magic than she would ever learn, but that was all done now, and he belonged at home in their safe cave in the forest.

Then came the morning in deep winter when Liva woke in bear form to find the hound at the entrance to the cave, staring into the morning light. The bear was nowhere to be seen.

"Is he gone to the river?" asked Liva, surprised because it had been weeks since he had gone that far from the cave. He must have been feeling very well indeed.

"No," said her mother.

"Then where?"

Her mother did not answer.

Liva felt a sick twist in her stomach, and her throat was so dry that her words cracked. "He will be back soon," she said, her voice as plaintive as it had been when she was very young. "Won't he?"

Her mother turned around, and Liva could see the truth in her red-rimmed hound's eyes.

No, it could not be. Liva began to rock back and forth, keening.

Her mother leaned over and whispered, "It is well."

But it was not well!

"He is old," said Liva. "It is dangerous. There are humans." Was that not what her father had told her? To stay away from humans and be safe?

But the hound said only, "Whatever the dangers are, they are his to face. This is his choice. He has ignored the calls of those in need for many months."

"But I do not want him to go. I need him," said Liva, though she would never have admitted such a thing if he had remained behind.

Her mother limped closer to Liva, but Liva threw herself back against the rock walls of the cave, heedless of the bruises that rose up under her bear hide. Then she ran out past her mother, into the forest and the bitter wind that took away all scent of her father's trail.

She looked toward the stream by the cave for marks in the ground. Downstream or up? She looked for broken branches from trees that her father had passed under lately. There—was that one? Or was that one there? She could not see with the wind and the tears in her eyes. She began to howl.

Then she took a breath and forced herself to hold it until her chest burned. When she let it out, she felt her claws, one at a time, each gust of wind as it hit her square in the chest, each tear as it froze on her fur. She had to think. She had to give up being a child. Her father needed her. She was old enough now. She had to be.

She turned to the right. The bear must have gone south. There was nothing to the north, no humans, no danger. She began to run, moving as quickly as possible. Though her father had left hours before, he could not travel as swiftly as she could. She held out hope that she might yet catch up to him.

She ran into the darkest part of the forest, heading due south toward the human village she had never been to. When the trees thinned, she began to walk along the river that led out of the mountains, into a blinding snow. Liva used her magic to quest out for any hint of her father. It was difficult to track his aur-magic, since he had no more than any other animal, but his pattern was as familiar to her as the smell of her mother.

There it was! A shape that glowed like a fluorescent moss, with a core of pain and exhaustion surrounded by flickers of intense determination. She could tell that he was south of her, by the river, traveling fast. He must be pushing himself very hard, beyond his own strength, and he did not stop.

The next moment she lost him in the storm. But she did not turn back. She wrapped herself in the warmth of her magic, pulling it around her shoulders, hips, and knees like a blanket of wool. For an hour or two, it worked. She could hear the river and smell it, and she picked her way over the shoreline, sometimes rock, sometimes sand.

When she became so cold that her legs went numb, she used her magic to bring sensation back to them. Her paws, too, needed magic to keep warm and moving. Liva was not stinting in her use of it. She spread it all over, until the ground around her was wet and muddy with bits of plant shoots showing above the ground, though nearby it was still covered in snow.

When the storm broke, she settled in for the night next to a boulder, and let herself drift to sleep. She woke only when she was shivering, and then just long enough to pour more magic around herself.

In the morning she woke comfortable and very warm.

But there was a snuffling sound close by.

Dozens of animals were snuggled in around her: dormice, a mink, a mole, three ferrets, a handful of shrews, several badgers, a lynx, a fawn, a newborn hare—still blind—several foxes, twin wolves, and a felfrass, among others.

She could feel how the animals pressed against her, not only with their bodies, but with their magic, trying to match her brightness with their own. They had come to her, despite her bear's shape, drawn by the wild aurmagic that pooled around her, attracted as though to water in a dry spell.

The more magic she pressed at them, urging them to retreat, the more they crowded her. They jostled one another for position closest to her, and one of the dormice was killed by a ferret, teeth against teeth.

Liva could do nothing to stop them from following

her, short of killing them.

She sighed, then let them come to her, making as much space for them as she could by the boulder, where her magic had melted snow and wakened grass and flowers underneath. The plants would die when she left, frozen by the winter's return.

Liva did not know what to do. When she reached her father, perhaps he would know how to undo what she had done with the aur-magic, how to detach these animals and send them back where they belonged. She felt humbled now, not as sure of herself as she had been.

After several efforts, Liva found her feet and began walking again along the river as it tumbled down small hills, making waterfalls and rapids of white water that she stopped to stare at, in awe of the beauty of a part of the forest she had never seen before.

As she moved south, the storm grew less fierce, but she was joined by more animals. She had to cross over the river at a narrowing, to skirt by the crumbling shelf on the other side. She took the form of an elk and stepped into the water.

The animals jumped in with her, all of them.

Liva gasped as the cold swallowed her up to her knees. The river water felt like liquid snow. Even her aur-magic could not protect her from the bite.

A shrew was swept away beside her, and then a badger. They simply stopped fighting the current and went floating downstream. Liva could feel the smallest hint of their magic as they bobbed furiously on the surface, and then they were gone.

Disgusted, she threw herself out of the river as soon as she could do so without magic, in the form of a pika, a creature like a mouse.

Lying facedown on the bank, she stirred to the sound of human voices.

Chapter Six

Jens

"What in the name of life and death are these doing here?" shouted Torus, waving his arm at a strange grouping of animals, all in a circle at the edge of the river.

Jens stared at the animals and could think of no explanation. He had never seen such a group all together. Were the flesh eaters and the plant eaters at peace? Perhaps the snowstorm had made them all confused? But their eyes were wide and bright.

"I don't care why they're here. Think of it as a gift. We'll kill them and take their skins back. Then we'll be men," said Harald, stroking his scraggly, red beard. He was two years younger than Jens, only fourteen, but he liked to pretend he was older.

"What if it's a trap?" asked Jens. "To be safe, we should leave these here and go after others."

"Safe? We've been hunting for four days in this storm,

44

with not a sight nor sound of animals. Now it's clear and we have a chance. If we don't bring something back now, we'll all go hungry," said Torus. This year the winter had been long and harsh, and more than half of the animals in the village had already been slaughtered. The land had grown less and less productive in recent years, and there were no stores of grain left in the village. If the hunters of the village did not find food in the forest, the village would be doomed.

"There's something wrong with these animals. They are not acting as they should," said Jens.

"When they're dead, they will taste just like any other animals," said Harald.

"And so many at once," said Torus. "Think how many days we will be able to eat. And what a celebration the village will throw for us!"

"I am not sure," said Jens. He was the oldest of them all and had been on the most hunts. But he was not surprised that they did not listen to him.

"What do *you* know?" Torus taunted Jens, for his lack of the tehr-magic was no secret. "The animals feel fine to me."

"No," Jens muttered distractedly. He was staring intently at the animals. He had no magic, but he felt something that was different. At the center of all the animals Jens could see a small creature almost like a mouse. No, it was a pika, black and white with shining eyes that turned and stared back at Jens as if pleading for its life.

45

I can't speak to you, Jens thought. *I can't hear you, either. I'm useless to help you.*

But then the pika disappeared in the flurrying snow around the river. The other animals moved sluggishly, as if to follow, but they did not move quickly enough.

"Leave them be!" Jens tried one more time.

But Harald cried out, "Kill! Hunt! Kill! The animals are ours."

The other boys whooped in excitement. "Ours! Ours!"

"If we die, we die as men. We die with honor!" shouted Torus, who was always trying to prove that he was no coward. In his effort to make sure of it, he sometimes brought danger to those around him.

Torus took out his sword and began to bellow.

The others took out their weapons—daggers and knives—for they did not have the coin that Torus's family did. Jens had only a slingshot. His father had refused to give Jens a knife after what had happened to his stone blade years ago.

The others began to shout to frighten the animals.

"I will cut you to pieces!"

"You can't run from me!"

"Dead! You will be dead!"

They charged forward.

A mink was killed and flung over Harald's shoulder. Then a raccoon, and a ferret. Jens found himself downstream along the banks of the river, though he had not meant to go so far, and he picked up a lynx, its white belly stained red.

There were dozens of carcasses scattered on the white snow, steaming with blood, and it seemed wrong to Jens. If they had come across a herd of deer or antelope, the hunting party would have killed one or two and left the rest. Here had been a massacre. This felt vicious, though it was true that those who were hungry in the village would not object to eating so much fresh meat.

Torus passed him and patted him on the shoulder. "Good for you. I wondered if you would turn back at the sight of blood. Your father says . . ." He stopped and gestured at the lynx on Jens's shoulder. "But here is the proof he is wrong. You will only need some more practice, and any hunting party will take you gladly."

Jens realized that Torus thought Jens had killed the lynx himself. He expected at any moment for one of the other young men to insist that the lynx was rightly his kill, but they all had so many carcasses to carry that no one argued. Jens began to suspect as they trudged back to the village that the others did not even remember which animals they had killed. For all their tehr-magic, they did not any of them think of one creature as different from another.

Jens shivered and moved the lynx to his other side so that he would not get a cramp. The body had already gone stiff in the cold.

Around him Jens listened to a hunting song and the

47

congratulations of one hunter to the next. As if they had done something remarkable in killing animals that had not even tried to escape death.

Jens thought of the small pika and was careful to check to see if any of the dead creatures were that one. Somehow it had escaped when the others had not, and Jens was glad of it. At least there was some life to rejoice in still.

CHAPTER SEVEN
Liva

LIVA CIRCLED BACK in the direction the humans had gone. She told herself she would return to tracking her father in a moment, but something inside her compelled her to follow the boy with the white-blond hair. He was taller now, but she recognized him right away. Jens, the one who had seen through her animal skin when she had been following the felfrass kit. He had been a member of a hunting party then, too. With humans, but not at all like them.

As a pika, she was small and low to the ground, black and white like dirty snow and nearly invisible. She followed the humans past the river, along a wide trail of trampled snow, blood, and noise.

She stopped at the first sight of the human village. All around it the forest had been cleared away. There were a few bony animals corralled by fences, sheep and goats and aurochsen, some of them with shelters to retreat to, others curled around stones or pressed against the human habitations. Smoke rose from the chimneys.

Liva felt acutely uncomfortable in this human place. Everything seemed wrong. The tehr-magic had a sour, rotten taste. She had never had to be this close to the way the humans took and corrupted the aur-magic for their own purposes.

She called out softly to the few animals fenced in here, but they did not respond. Liva had heard stories from her father of tame animals, how they forgot their own language and learned to be more human. Her father had told her that the animals chose this, that there were benefits for them in the relationship. But Liva could not see how it was possible. She wanted to set all the animals free, even if they might die in the forest. She wanted to teach them to speak again as wild animals spoke She wanted to take their tehr-magic and make it aur-magic again, but she did not know how.

Liva sniffed her way forward until she reached a large building in the center of the village. There were sounds inside, not just human voices, but rhythmic thumping and something like the call of birds. There was an opening, a small crack in the wood, and she peered in, then nudged her way inside.

The humans were dancing around the stripped and smoking animal flesh. Some of the younger ones she recognized from the hunt; they wore animal skins over their shoulders, not yet cured, and they had blood smeared onto their faces. They laughed and copied different mating calls. But there was no real wildness in their eyes, only the imitations of it.

Was this what it was to be human?

She strained, leaning forward, then stepped away from the wall.

Suddenly, a hand swooped down and picked her up. Liva squirmed, surprised that she had been caught so easily, without any warning through the aur-magic. She could not get away unless she used magic to change her form, and she feared the consequences of that in this human village, so she held back for the moment.

The boy who held her did so without anger, without pain. She looked up to his face, wondering what human would treat an animal so well.

Of course. She should have known it from the lack of any magic at all.

It was Jens.

Liva stopped struggling, and slowly he opened his hand. With one finger he petted her cheek. "I know you," he whispered.

"I know you," Liva eeped at him in the language of the pika. He could not know what she meant, but he nodded in response.

"What is it, Jens?" asked one of the other humans who had killed the animals in the forest.

A human with the tehr-magic, Liva felt clearly, disliking him.

Jens tried to close his hand around Liva again, but it was too late.

The other human had snatched her up and held her high.

"Stomping game!" he shouted.

Liva heard the anger in his voice as he directed his look at Jens. It was like an animal challenging another, but without any joy of life, and far more viciousness.

"No!" said Jens. He flung his fist into the other human's face, and Liva felt herself falling.

She was back in Jens's hand in a moment, and shivered there.

"It's only a mouse," said the human who was pulling himself off the floor, his face beginning to show a livid bruise where he had been struck by Jens.

"A pika, idiot Torus," said Jens.

"Doesn't matter. Just as good for stomping. It will run, won't it?"

A part of Liva wished she were home with her mother at that moment, that she had never thought to go after her father, and had never seen the hunting party of humans.

But Jens was so different. He reminded her of a fierce mother bear, protecting a child. But at the same time, he was like a wolf with hackles raised, growling low, giving a snake the chance to slink away from marked territory.

How could he have no aur-magic?

"You've killed enough today, I would think," said

Jens, gesturing toward the smoking animal meats.

"That's meat," said Torus. "Not fun."

"I'll give you fun," said Jens.

Liva felt a chill run through her, and even the humans hushed.

But not for long. Soon Liva could hear whispers growing. "Torus, Torus, Torus!" they called.

No one rooted for Jens.

He was the lone wolf here. The one who had lost his pack and his home but was still ready to fight. It was in the way he lifted his head against the odds, and how he held his shoulders high and let his eyes dart about.

In one swift movement, he tucked Liva into a pouch wrapped around his middle. It was dark and warm, and in it was a large white feather threaded with silver. Liva put her nose against it and felt thrilled by the burst of aur-magic. It rarely happened that birds let their feathers fall without taking back the magic in them first. But a bird with a great deal of the aur-magic might not notice.

Torus taunted Jens.

Jens seemed to dance back and forth.

Torus threw a punch at Jens. Then another.

Inside the pouch, Liva was jostled as Jens staggered backward.

Liva tried to send magic to him, to heal him more quickly. She dared not send too much, for it would be too obvious to the other humans that it was not a natural healing. But the magic she sent to him seemed to slide right through him and was taken up by other humans. Made into more tehr-magic, never to be returned. As if there were not already too much inside this building.

Jens got to his feet and put up his hands in fists.

Liva braced herself.

"Jens!" shouted one loud voice. "Jens, smash him! Make him sorry he ever touched you!"

Jens tried to swing at Torus's face, but the other boy slipped underneath the blow, then came back with a kick at Jens's knee.

Liva heard a cracking sound, and Jens went down hard.

"Get up, boy!" came the same voice from the crowd. "Don't let him beat you!"

Torus was already circling the center of the building, his hands held high above his head, a picture of victory.

"Torus! Torus!" the crowd cheered relentlessly.

Jens got up on one foot. He made a loud heaving sound, and with each breath, there was a whimper of pain.

"Move!" shouted the voice. "Show yourself a man now!"

Liva focused her senses on the voice. Whoever he was had a great deal of the tehr-magic, gleaned from countless animal deaths.

Then Jens hopped forward, bouncing Liva in the pouch, drawing her attention back to the fight.

"Try it. You know I'm stronger than you are, and

I always will be," Torus said, arms across his chest in invitation.

Torus was no more than a shrieking magpie, Liva thought in fury. If only Liva could have shown him her bear form. Then they would see who was afraid and who was not. Jens would stand firm and Torus would be cowering in fear.

"I do not want to hurt you," said Jens.

"Then that is the difference between us. You will never be a hunter if you do not learn to be ruthless."

"And you will never have any true friends. They will all be waiting to hurt you when you are weak." Jens tried to put weight on his injured leg and grimaced in pain.

Torus stepped forward. "Here, let me help you, friend," he said with a sly grin. Quickly, he tugged Jens off balance.

There was applause from the other humans in the audience.

"Useless!" shouted the voice. At last Liva got a glimpse of the face of the man with dark tehr-magic. She was startled to see that he had white-blond hair, just like Jens did. In fact, his face was similar to Jens's in many ways. The same jutting chin, the same light eyes, the same flushed cheeks.

His father.

But there was none of the love in his eyes that Liva had seen in both her mother's black hound eyes and her father's bear eyes. How could there be with such poison held inside of him?

Jens winced at his father's voice, then took a breath and steadied himself.

He breathed out and in.

Then he clenched his fist, drew it back, and flung it forward with all the force he had, striking Torus in the chest. The punch would have done damage on its own, but Liva added aur-magic to it. Only a little, and only at the last moment. She told herself she was only making the battle more fair.

Liva could feel her aur-magic slam into Torus and rip through him. It was moving too quickly for him to take it into himself, and it tore out some of his own tehr-magic with it.

Torus took in a great, gasping breath of air. His mouth opened, but no words came out of it. He waved his arms, then slumped to the floor, his eyes rolling back in his head.

None of the humans seemed to notice that aur-magic had been used. Liva was relieved—that danger occurred to her only after the fact.

There was a brief silence, followed by "Jens! Jens! Jens!" shouted in precisely the way that those same humans had shouted "Torus!" a moment earlier.

Jens's father came forward and clapped him on the back. This made Jens stagger in pain. "I never thought I'd see the day, boy." He pushed Jens's head down, then let go of it suddenly. "Time to celebrate," he said, heading to the corner—and the vats of ale. He didn't take Jens with him, however.

Jens gently let himself down onto the ground and crawled toward Torus.

Liva wanted to shout at him to stop, that Torus deserved what he had gotten. But Jens proved himself kinder than she was. Liva could think of no animal who would have gone back to check on the health of the loser in a battle. As for the other humans, they had lost interest in the fight now that it was over, and they did not try to help Torus, either.

As Jens leaned forward, Liva was able to raise her nose out of the pouch and sniff at Torus. There was something wrong with him more than just the loss of his tehr-magic.

He was not breathing.

The aur-magic Liva had forced into him had done more damage than she had thought. Humans were used to taking from animals, but Liva's magic was far stronger.

Jens put a hand out and touched Torus's caved-in chest. "I did not mean to do this," he said softly. And he looked down at Liva.

She shrank back from his sight, not wanting to admit that it was her fault, not his. She did not want him to despise her.

Gently Jens straightened Torus's head and neck in line with the rest of his body. He pressed his lips onto

Torus's and breathed into him.

This time, Liva used the aur-magic more carefully. She let out only a little bit, and directed it to flow into Torus's blood naturally, as if his heart were beating again. Then she pressed magic into his heart itself, to start it once more.

Liva would never have done this to an animal that had died. Death was part of the natural cycle of the true magic. To fight against it would have been to damage the integrity of the aur-magic itself. But this was an unnatural death, so Liva felt that she needed to reverse what she had done.

Suddenly Torus's head yanked forward. He coughed, then took a breath. And another.

Liva had not healed his chest wound, which bled again, but she had done enough. She hoped that Torus would not be able to tell easily that she had altered the magic in him. He was not full of tehr-magic now, but had a bit of the aur-magic that flowed in and out with the forest and the animals. Perhaps he would get used to it. Perhaps he would even come to like it.

But at the moment he was angry.

"Get away from me!" said Torus when his eyes flickered open to see Jens's face. Jens pulled away, and Torus convulsed, his face red. He turned to the side and vomited up a great deal of pale-colored fluid. Finally he tottered to his feet and threw himself away from Jens and out of the building.

So much for her one attempt to save humans from their own magic, Liva thought.

Jens remained on the floor, staring at his knee.

Liva watched him. He was the one who deserved her intervention. *He* was a human she would want to save. But her aur-magic didn't touch him at all! It made no sense that there could be a human whom neither kind of magic could touch.

She tried to send aur-magic to him again, thinking that she needed to send less and hold it for him until he took it in. If he had some injury to his magic, perhaps from when he was a child, then he might have forgotten how to hold it.

But it was the same as before. She held it, but he never took it in, and when she let it go, it was gone into the world around him.

Liva tried to think what else might have happened to his natural sense for magic. If he hated tehr-magic the way she did, perhaps he had pushed it away too often. In that case, she would need to give him a great deal of aur-magic, but pressed directly into his knee.

Liva guided the aur-magic as precisely as she could this time, then held it in place, but it was no use. It went through Jens and was useless, as before. He had not even noticed that it was there.

He must have been born without magic of any kind. Perhaps his mother lacked magic, too? Obviously, his father did not.

Liva heard Jens sigh next to her. He had pulled both his legs close to himself and leaned against the wall of the building. He took Liva out of the pouch and placed her on his hand.

"What do I do with you now?" he asked.

"Take me back to the woods," Liva eeped at him. "And you come with me, too. Don't stay here. Not with humans." Even lacking magic, Jens belonged more in the woods than in the human village.

But Jens did not understand. "You make me doubt myself. Are you who I think you are or not?" he said.

Before she could answer, Liva felt herself snatched up by an unfamiliar hand.

CHAPTER EIGHT

Jens

"AH, HERE IS that mouse!" said Jens's father, holding Liva aloft. In his other hand he held a tankard of ale. "I wondered where it had gone."

"It is a pika," said Jens quietly. He dared not show his true feelings for the creature, nor let his father suspect what he thought was hidden beneath the mouselike form. Any villager would feel terror and disgust at the thought of a human who had aur-magic or who could use it to become an animal, but Jens thought his father would be worse than most.

"Torus was right. You don't know how to have a little fun," said his father. "You don't think of animals in the right way at all. They are ours, just as this one is. Ours to do with as we please. As food—or fun."

"No, Father!" said Jens desperately.

"It is only a pika. And you killed a lynx today already.

What difference does one more death make?"

Jens could not explain. It would only make things worse if he said that he had not killed the lynx. But at least the lynx had been smoked for its meat. This pika would be worth no effort for food or coat.

"Killing for no reason is wrong," he said urgently. "The animals may be ours, but if we kill too many of them, then what will become of us? There will be no animals left."

"This one animal will make no difference," said his father. "Now show me you are my son!" He whistled, and then there were seven men around him, shouting and poking at the quivering pika whom Jens's father flung on the floor. Liva leaped up just in time to avoid a booted foot coming for her. She darted this way and that, but the circle of feet was inescapable.

"Stop!" said Jens, and tried to dive for the pika, but in that moment she changed shape, soaring into the air in the form of an owl, with strong wings to launch her away from Jens's father and the others. A hoot filled the building as the owl rose into the smoke above the cooking fires, then flew up through the chimney and outside.

Jens stared in awe, his mouth open, his ears ringing. He had seen such a transformation twice before, from wolf to human to felfrass, but there was no getting used to it. It was amazing.

"Aur-magic!" shouted Jens's father.

"Aur-magic! After it!" shouted the other men.

They ran out of the gathering place and toward the forest, chasing the owl, whose shape was a distant and fleeting one in the sky. Jens followed quickly. He did not think they had a chance against an owl that could change shape once more, whenever it was necessary, but he could not be sure. He had to help her escape.

"Get your bows!" shouted one of the men to the boys who were still standing.

The boys ran for their bows and arrows. Jens moved toward them, deliberately getting in their way. They fell over his feet, then cursed him for his clumsiness. He managed to break at least one bow before the boys got away.

Jens ran after them into the forest. He could see no sign of the owl, but his father shouted, "I can sense the aur-magic. This way!"

They were headed north, which was where Jens had first met the girl Liva.

Jens could not allow them to continue in that direction. He saw a bird flying overhead and shouted, "This way!" It was the wrong color and shape, but it was similar enough that at least half the party turned immediately, rushing in the other direction.

What arrows were left went to bring down that bird. It was a small hawk, and the rest of the party, including Jens's father, came back when it was downed.

Jens stood over the still body of the hawk and felt the weight of this death on his hands. He had never killed an animal before.

And it was not his bow and arrow that had downed this one. But his intent had. He'd done it so that Liva could escape. He would have traded her for any animal in the forest, of any size. But the hawk had been beautiful. It still was, even in death.

"The aur-magicked one did not change into a *hawk*," said his father stubbornly, staring at it.

"It must have," said Jens, quietly.

"It was an owl. I saw it. And far whiter than this one."

"You must be mistaken," said Jens.

"And there is no sign of the aur-magic in this one that would allow it to change from mouse to bird," his father went on.

But the other men seemed less interested in finding the real creature who had changed shape and more interested in enjoying their triumph.

They took up the hawk and brought it back to the village, intending for it to be stuffed and raised as a reminder to all about what happened to those who used aur-magic.

"Aur-magic," his father muttered as they marched. "The Hunter would know the difference between an animal and a human with aur-magic. That's what the burning is for."

Jens shivered at the thought of Liva burning.

"We are too far north, too much away from the strong tehr-magic of the the city. Your mother wanted to come here. I never understood why. She loved the untouched forest and its wild animals, aur-magic and all. But I should have gone back the day she died. Not that it would have made any difference with you."

"Father, I like it here," said Jens.

"Because you can't tell any more difference between the aur-magic and the tehr-magic than you can between an owl and a hawk," said his father, and with a cutting hand gesture made it clear that he did not want Jens to follow him back to the gathering place.

Jens went instead to his hut, glad that he had seen the pika, but a little disappointed that he had not seen the girl. Ah well, he would not wish Liva back into the danger of the village. If he wished to see her again, he would have to go to her. Alone, without a hunting party. He wondered whether he would be able to find his way that far north safely. The animals there were not naturally afraid of humans, and he had no magic to tame them.

But as he approached his hut, he saw the owl circling overhead, and his heart pinched inside his chest. It was not that he had thought she had been harmed, but it was so good to see her again, to know that she cared for him enough to return, even after all that had happened to her. She knew that he was not like the other village men, and that made all the difference to Jens.

As soon as he thought of the other village men, he remembered her danger. He stepped out into the clear and waved urgently at the owl, thinking to send her away.

Instead of obeying him, the owl flew to the ground next to his door and in a moment was in the form of a pika once again—less noticeable than a strange human girl if a villager passed by. And if Jens's father saw her, he would know the truth and tell the others to kill her.

The pika ran up his leg, licking gently at the knee that was starting to swell. Already it strained against his leggings.

"What do you want?" Jens asked.

The pika eeped at him.

Jens tried. "You want food?" he guessed.

The pika eeped even more loudly.

Which probably meant he'd gotten it wrong.

He dared not take her into his hut in case his father returned, but they would have a little shelter in the animal lean-to. "Come here," Jens said, beckoning.

The pika followed him into the lean-to as he sat and put his back to the wood. She danced around him as a pika, then changed at last into her human form, into Liva.

Jens stared at her, then offered her a coarsely woven blanket on the floor, embarrassed. He had remembered the awe he felt in her presence, but not the particulars of her beauty. She had dark hair and dark eyes and a quick, delicate way of moving. In some ways, she was more animal than human. But in another way, Jens thought he had never met a human who had seemed more sure of herself. *Liva.* He said the name again in his mind and savored the taste.

She wrapped the blanket around her shoulders, then knelt at his side and put a hand to his wounded knee.

Jens tried not to wince away from her touch, and almost succeeded.

"I've just tried again to heal your leg with my magic," she said after a time, "but it did not work. I do not know how to help you."

"I have no magic," Jens said. He could not see any reason why a girl with such power would have anything to do with him. But he felt so different in her eyes, as if she saw something no one else could—as if merely being with her made him better.

"I know," said Liva impatiently. "But I had hoped—" She touched the leg again. Her eyes closed, and she seemed to be concentrating, but Jens could feel no change in his pain.

He breathed through clenched teeth, then heard her let out a long sigh.

She shook her head. "No. I do not understand it. How can you be so empty of magic?"

If anyone else had said the same thing to him, Jens would have taken offense. But she stared at him with complete honesty in her eyes.

"Does it matter so much to you?" Jens asked. He had been shamed by this all his life. Did it have to be the first thing she, too, thought of when she saw him?

"It matters to me because it isn't fair. Of all humans, why should you be the one who lacks magic? Any magic, not just the aur-magic. I have tried to sneak it into you, to throw it, to press it, to hold it for you. Nothing works."

"I've never had magic, and I've accepted that," said Jens. "I can't calm the animals. I can't kill them. But there are other things I can do that are useful in the village."

"I don't mean—" She stopped. "I hate the tehr-magic they have here, in the village. That is not what I would want for you either."

"Only the aur-magic," said Jens.

She stared at him. "Of course. It is the true magic, the original magic. The magic that was born from the link between humans and animals. It is life itself. But humans take it and form it into what they think is useful to them. Tehr-magic." There was disdain in her voice.

"If you could give me the aur-magic, then I would have to leave," said Jens. "They would sense it, and the aur-magic is not tolerated here." Though sometimes he hated his life in the village so much anything seemed it would be better.

"Do you know what happened? How you lost all sense for magic?"

Jens shrugged. "I was born this way. I used to think my lack of magic must have come from my mother. She died when I was born. But my father has told me so often that I would be a disappointment to her. So there must be a different reason. I wonder sometimes—"

"What?" asked Liva.

Yes, thought Jens. *I will tell her what I have never told anyone else.* "If my lack of magic was what killed her. If she saw me and could not bear to live with a son who had no magic at all. Or if it was the fact that I somehow stole the magic out of her when I was born, until she died."

"No," said Liva softly. "That is not possible."

"How can you be sure?" said Jens. He had not realized how much this would matter to him.

Liva pointed to a long scar on her leg. Jens noticed then how many other scars she had, running up arms and legs to the torso hidden behind the blanket.

"This one came from when I was only a few months old. I wanted to be a jay, and so I changed myself. I had used the aur-magic many times before, but not enough that I could immediately fly without falling. My mother had to come for me and carry me back to the cave in her teeth." She turned her neck to the side and showed a row of scars there, tiny dots that looked like many rows of teeth pressed against her skin.

"Your mother?" asked Jens.

"She and my father gifted me with a great wealth of aur-magic when I was born."

"But I thought you said—," said Jens, feeling sick at heart.

"It's impossible to die from giving up too much magic voluntarily. Creatures can give up what extra they have, and live with only what other animals or humans have. My mother chose to turn herself into a hound before she gave up her magic, so that she could protect me," said Liva.

"And your father?" asked Jens.

"He changed himself into a bear so that he too could protect me as well as any other humans he believed were worthy of it."

"He protects humans with aur-magic?" said Jens.

"Yes," said Liva. "Because they are the most vulnerable. You, on the other hand, with your lack of magic—think of how dangerous you would be in the forest."

"I think you are teasing me," said Jens stiffly.

"Not at all. Without either aur-magic or tehr-magic, you would be invisible to animals. You would not even have to move silently for them to ignore you."

Jens thought about this for a long moment. "Are you sure of this?"

"I have been testing you," said Liva. "I am as sure as I can be. Don't you trust me when it comes to magic?"

Jens had no reason not to trust her. And he would think about what she said. Truly, he would. But it was a great deal to take in at once—that his lack of magic might be an asset rather than a defect. That his whole life might be different, if he lived in the forest rather than a village.

Changing the subject, he said, "You are very lucky, to live in a place where you are valued."

"Yes," she said, with her head bowed. "Yes, I am." Then she looked up at him and he felt as though he would be happy if he never saw another face in his life.

"I would have thought that you could heal yourself with your magic, so that you would have no scars," Jens said, his mouth very dry.

"Ah, but what fun would there be in that? My scars remind me of stories I might forget, and every animal is proud of its scars."

"And every human," said Jens, thinking of his father's pride in scars after hunting.

"Ah. Humans, too?" asked Liva. "Then perhaps I should not try again to heal your leg, in hopes that it will give you a good scar?"

"It is not the scarring I am worried about. It is the damage beneath that might lame me. Animals do not admire the infirm, do they?"

"No," said Liva shortly. There was a flash in her eyes, and Jens knew that he had touched something tender in her, but he did not know what it was. "How can you bear to live here with the humans in this village? They are so cruel, so unnatural."

"I suppose I have always thought this is what I deserved," said Jens.

She shook her head. "Not what you deserve. Not at all. You should be far away from them."

"I do not know if I am strong enough to live alone." There. He had admitted it. She made him feel stronger, but not strong enough.

Liva smiled. "But in the forest, one is never alone.

71

There are always creatures around. Ants, worms, gnats, beetles, if nothing else. And the sun itself, the clouds, the wind, the trees that sigh, the trickle of the water as it flows, the taste of the changing seasons."

"And all of them apart from me. Perhaps I do not belong anywhere."

She laughed, without a hint of sadness. "Neither do I. I like it that way. I go where I please. I am free."

How Jens envied her. "Well, I thank you for your attempt to help me with your aur-magic," he said. He could not bring himself to tell her to leave, however it would be to her benefit. He wanted her to stay with him through the night and into the morning, and listen to her for long hours. It was not just the information that he craved, but the way she acted toward him. He had never been treated so well before in his life.

Liva tilted her head to one side, just like an owl.

"You should keep the knee cold, to keep it from swelling," Liva said.

His knee? Oh, yes. He had almost forgotten about it. Now the pain came back, and with it, the sense of his own limitations.

"I think I am already cold enough." Jens had goose bumps up and down his limbs, though he was not yet shaking, thanks to the lean-to.

She bent down and tried to pack some snow around his knee, gathered from the outside edge of the lean-to.

He yelped in pain. He had seen men die from such

wounds before. It was the swelling that did it, for it ran through their whole bodies.

Then she let go of the ball of snow and stared at the ground with the same look of concentration she had shown before, when she had tried to give him her aur-magic. In a moment, Jens felt a strange sensation. It was cold, but not freezing.

He pulled himself upright in surprise, but slowly relaxed into it as the pain drifted away and he could breathe again without thinking of it.

"What did you do?" he asked, staring back and forth at her and his own knee. It could not heal so quickly, surely!

"I can't send magic into you, for some reason, but I can send it into the snow to warm it. The energy that is released is not magical, but physical. And your leg will take that."

"Oh," said Jens, as if he understood what she meant. The pain left him and he felt light-headed, as if he could float away. "Thank you," he said, or thought he said, though he could not be sure. His lips had moved, but he could not seem to hear any sounds that came out of them. Or sounds anywhere.

It was wonderful.

Liva kept doing whatever she did with the magic until she could touch his knee without him noticing. It was still slightly swollen, but he found that he could walk on it normally. "You won't regret it, now, will you? That I healed you and you'll have no mark to remember the fight with another human?"

Jens glanced up quickly, but saw her mouth was twisted, teasing. "No," he said. "No regrets at all." He felt hot now, rather than cold, and was about to turn away when Liva leaned forward. He tried to turn to her to meet her kiss, but she ended up planting her kiss on his ear.

She laughed then. "I've heard of human kisses. My father tells stories. But they seem easier in my imagination."

Jens was too flustered to speak for a long moment.

"Thank you for saving me when those men tried to kill me," said Liva, with a step backward.

"You saved yourself," Jens whispered.

"I think not entirely. If I had, then those men would still be in the forest, chasing after me. And they are not. You are one who gives life rather than taking it. Do you see how you stand above the others?"

Jens shrugged.

"And you did not kill any of those animals who followed me by the river, did you? I think I would be able to smell the death on you, if you had."

"I should have tried to save them as well," said Jens. "But I could not think how."

"Animals die," she said.

"In that, we are the same," said Jens.

"In more than that."

Jens wondered whether she would kiss him again, but

she changed back into an owl and the blanket dropped to the floor. He watched as the owl flew toward the south without turning back or making a sound. But she had been there. The improvement in his leg proved that.

He watched her fly away and turned to enter the hut. Seeing something fluttering on the ground, he bent down and picked it up. An owl feather, speckled with black and white in as distinct a pattern as the snowbird's white threaded with silver. He turned it over in his fingers with a smile before adding it to his pouch and returning to his hut. His father would be home soon, but for now he could think of her and imagine that she was still with him.

When he woke in the morning, his father was shouting at him to get up and go to the stream for water to boil for breakfast. Jens went for it, his leg much better, and he thought of the girl who had done it and how nothing else mattered.

Chapter Nine
Liva

*L*IVA FLEW FAST, making her way south back over the river. She saw no bear tracks and felt no trace of her father's magic. She might have to be closer to him to sense him. She hoped that he was well. She had not meant to stay that long with Jens, but time had slipped so quickly away. She could not stop thinking about the boy even now.

She tried to think of an animal form for Jens that would be fitting. He was as protective as a bear, as tender as a doe, and as smart as an eagle. He should be in a form that could soar—and he should sing, for his voice fell on her ears like music.

But his village and his own father treated him terribly, all because he had none of the tehr-magic. Liva was glad he did not, for she did not think she could love anyone who used magic selfishly like that.

She dove down to a stream and changed into human

form to drink and rest. She liked the form more now than ever, despite the cold. Jens had recognized her as the pika and as the owl, but they could only speak together when she was human, and she loved how she felt when they talked. She cupped her hands, splashed icy water over her face, then leaned back against the rocks to watch the clouds in the sky move by.

It was then that Liva saw the great shadow of the bird.

Liva stopped to look up at it, and then she could not move. It was beautiful, its white feathers glinting with silver underneath its wings, and its sheer size made her feel faint. Larger than any bird she had seen, it seemed to be coming just for her, for it flew directly overhead. Compared with the aur-magic in this snowbird, Liva's was a drop of water against a storm. She felt like sobbing out her empty sorrow as the bird passed by, casting a huge shadow over her, but she could not speak at all.

Liva flew through the night and stopped only when she heard a bellowing at the break of dawn. She felt blindly in her magic for the source.

It was some distance away, but hot and familiar.

Her father.

She flew toward him, glad at last that the storm had gone and the sky was clear. She called out to tell her father that she was coming for him, but he did not answer her.

When she was close enough to see the blood dripping

from his neck, Liva could tell he was badly wounded. He staggered forward, making inarticulate sounds.

Who had attacked him? Men from the village? But they could never have passed her. And for her father to be wounded so, with his experience and his size, there had to have been many humans involved.

But the closer that Liva came to him, the stranger—and colder—the wound seemed.

He did not seem to recognize her, even when she swooped down from the air and changed into bear form before his eyes.

He moved jerkily and in circles, as if he had lost all sense of direction. He muttered to himself, and when Liva put a paw to him, she felt the same lack of magic she had felt in Jens.

She had to give him back some of her inheritance of aur-magic. Her mother had refused to accept it when she was wounded, but the hound had not been in such danger of dying. The bear most definitely was.

"Father!" she shouted at him to get his attention.

She only succeeded in making him roar at her and swing a paw in her direction. It would have hit her in the face if she had not ducked. This massive, threatening bear was not anything like the gentle father she had always known.

She could feel how the aur-magic had been cut from him at his neck. But when it poured out, it disappeared as if it had never been. It did not return to the forest. Liva could not understand how this could be.

Blood still flowed from the bear's wound. If she could bring the edges of the wound together—gently, so that her father's system was not shocked, perhaps he could hold enough aur-magic inside him to heal the inner wounds.

Liva let her aur-magic flow out of her like a breeze. She waited for it to make the bear calm, no more than that. Once he could stop threatening her, she could give him more.

But the aur-magic moved right past him, not rejected as it had been with her mother—simply reabsorbed back into the woods behind him.

Panicked, Liva shaped her aur-magic like an arrow that was aimed for the bear's heart.

Again, the magic simply went through him.

Just as it had with Jens, no matter what she had tried.

Liva's face stung with tears. The effort she'd used made her feel sick. Her balance was gone, and she had to put a paw out to a nearby rock to hold herself steady.

Trying to calm herself, Liva tried a third time.

She blasted out all the aur-magic she could in one burst. But as soon as it was gone, she knew it had been in vain. She watched as the trees behind the bear grew buds on their branches, brief bits of spring that would not last.

She felt as weak as a new cub. She had to breathe

through her mouth to get in enough air to keep herself from blacking out.

She ambled close to her father and put a paw on his leg.

But he threw her off and fell to the ground, rolling from side to side, as any ordinary bear in a rage might. This could not be her father!

Liva stood back and watched him with her magic senses acutely alert. The bear had bled off so much aur-magic that he tasted to her as empty as Jens had been, and the state was irreversible. But it made no sense, for Liva had become convinced by Jens that what had happened to him was a fluke of birth, like a snake born with two heads, or a moose calf born without its two hind legs. She had not thought there was any hand behind it.

Now she knew better. Humans had changed aur-magic to tehr-magic. They must have done this as well.

In a flash of heat, Liva knew she wanted revenge. She wanted to make whoever had done this moan as her father did. Not so long ago she had been proud to think herself grown up. Now she wanted to weep and to be held by her mother and comforted like a baby. This was too much for her.

She was supposed to have great aur-magic for some grand purpose, but Liva could think of nothing that would make her father's sacrifice worth anything.

She called out in the language of magic for help,

though she did not have any reason to believe she would be answered. But somehow it seemed only a few moments before she heard the bark of a hound.

She looked up and felt hope once more.

Her mother had come.

Chapter Ten

Jens

EIGHT BOYS WERE made men in the celebration the day after the hunt. Torus and Harald were among them. Jens was not. And he did not argue, for he did not care anymore.

The others painted themselves with the blood of the animal they had killed, then swallowed the vital organs raw. Liver, heart, lungs, and eyes. The tongue was reserved for last.

Afterward the newly made men linked arms and danced in front of the villagers. Then the girls and women were asked to leave, and it was time for a night of swaggering battles.

The youngest boys who remained were only four or five years old. It was meant to be a night of wildness and violence, a night meant to prove that next year's hunting season would be as successful as this year's. But Jens could feel no pride in this.

Instead he watched morosely as two brothers blood-
ied each other while their father encouraged more and
more violence.

Another young boy, no more than ten years old,
swung at Jens and took him by surprise.

He ducked.

In an instant he realized it was the wrong thing to do,
but there was no taking it back. The boy had expected
Jens to engage him. When Jens refused, it was taken as
an insult.

Jens gritted his teeth against the lingering pain in
his leg and tried to join another battle with Harald, as he
was closer to Jens in age and more likely to give him a
fair fight. But Harald ignored him completely. After all,
he was a man in the village now. Jens was not.

Jens told himself he should walk away, go home and
go to sleep. It was what only the old men did, and it would
invite others to call him a woman. But how much worse
could his reputation in the village become?

Liva. She would not admire him for fighting with
other humans. He would think of her tonight, and her
beautiful strength.

As he walked away, he heard laughter behind him.
And then his mother's name, Gudrun, and a guttural spit
and a curse on her for bearing such a son. Harald, who
had just refused a fight, was taunting him.

He could not bear it. It was one thing for him to suf-
fer, but his mother was defenseless. She had given her life

for him, and he would not hear her memory maligned.

Frustrated, he turned and swung as hard as he could, taking Harald off guard and knocking him to the ground. He would no longer be ignored. Harald's face was already purpling with the mark of Jens's hand. As Harald got to his feet and maneuvered closer, a group of men began to form a circle around them.

"Coward!" Jens heard, as he ducked one of Harald's blows. Harald was faster than Jens—except after a night of feasting and drinking like this one.

It was quiet in the building. Jens had seen fights before, and there were always onlookers calling out encouragement or disgust to both sides. Not now.

They did not think he was one of them.

Then came a blinding moment of realization: Jens was as alone here as he ever would be out in the forest. More alone, for in the village the animals were against him as well. Smoke stung his eyes. Harald was waiting for him to continue the fight, hands clenched into fists, stance ready for battle.

But Jens knew what he wanted, and it was not this life. Not another moment of it.

He took a step toward the open door. Harald was happy to see him go, raising his hand and shouting out his triumph to roars of approval.

Jens decided that he would leave without another word, the building, the village, this life.

Then his father stepped in front of him, large and

reeking. He had come to Jens's side at last.

"Do you wish to have your man's gift from me?" he asked.

Jens felt his breath catch in his throat, as thick as a piece of meat that he had not chewed well enough. A gift from his father? The tradition was that a father gave his son a gift at the ceremony of his manhood, to help him on his way in life, now that he would care for himself. Not having gone through the ceremony, Jens was not technically a man, and he was surprised that his father would make this offer. But for a moment, Jens believed it was true and relaxed, waiting.

Then out of the corner of his eye he saw his father's hand clench into a fist. It flew at him and connected with his jaw. Jens fell to the floor, and his head was filled with the sound of his father's laughter.

"That's the only gift you'll ever get from me."

Afterward, the carousing began again. Or had it ever stopped? Jens's father entered a wrestling match with another man without a glance back.

No one looked at Jens at all.

Painfully he got up and tottered outside. He welcomed the cold of the night on his cheeks, going as fast as he could to the edge of the village, limping a little on the side where his knee hurt still.

He stared up at the stars and marked out a northern constellation that could have been a snowbird with one wing folded.

Those are the edges of my new village, he told himself. He crossed the river when it grew light, and heard the sound of wolves crying out in the distance, as if they could already smell his blood. But he felt no fear, for he was going home at last.

CHAPTER ELEVEN

Liva

"**D**O NOT GIVE him your aur-magic!" the hound barked out harshly.

Liva was astonished. "He is dying," she said.

"Even so. He gave you the aur-magic for a reason. Do not undo what he gave up so much to accomplish." The hound stood between Liva and the bear, as if guarding him against his daughter.

"You do not even care that he is dying!" Liva accused her mother. This was not what she wanted when she called out for help.

"We all die," her mother said more gently. "That is the way of being mortal. Animals and humans, it makes us the same. Your father has never wished to escape from that. It is living this long that has been the most difficult for him. Think how he has outlived all others he has ever known, for the sake of saving the true magic. Will you make him sacrifice again, live longer again, despite his desire for rest? Only because you are afraid?"

Liva sobbed.

"He knew this time would come," her mother said.

"But he left without a word," said Liva. "At night."

"He thought it would be easier for you that way. It was only when I saw you leave the cave that I knew you had to make things difficult, and so I followed you for your own sake."

At this, Liva threw herself at her mother, a nearly grown bear cub against the full-grown but failing wild hound. Liva changed into the form of a hound herself, not thinking of anything but this moment, this battle. But her mother was ready for her and kept her position, all four paws on Liva's body, in just the right place to keep her immobile.

A wolf had no better effect, nor a moose, nor an elk.

Still furious, Liva tried to change into an eagle, with powerful talons to cut at her mother, but her claws caught only at the air. Her mother shifted position and tugged at her wings until Liva cried out at the pain and changed back into the bear cub she had been before.

That was when she felt the death of her father, in the sudden change of the magic all around her. His aur-magic had been draining out, but this last bit was palpable. It was like the last fall of a tree's leaves or the final stilling of a river frozen at the beginning of a bitterly cold winter. It was the last moment of sunset before it was night, the last call of a bird as it flew north, never to be heard from

again. It was the smallest of changes, yet it was everything.

Liva sagged and found that she had no strength for
weeping.

Her mother tried to snuggle next to her, but Liva
would have none of it.

"Tell me," she demanded, her voice harsh and bitter.
"Why should he die for those with the aur-magic? When
he had already given it up himself? Why should he go
to help humans, when he had given up being human as
well?"

"He would hear them call to him, those with the aur-
magic who had been accused, who were sentenced to
death," said the hound. "He could not ignore them."

"But he had given me his aur-magic."

The hound shook her head. "But not his responsibility. I told him that he should let it go, that he had no more
power to do the task. He should have waited for you to
take up the burden, but he said he could not allow you to
do so until you were ready, and that he was needed now.
I cannot say I was ashamed of him for that."

"And that night? Did he tell you who he was leaving
us for?" asked Liva bitterly.

"He told me he had dreamed of the same family for
weeks. A mother and a father and a young girl with an
affinity for bees.

"She had promised her parents to keep her aur-magic
a secret, for it was strong. They knew the risk of it, but

they had chosen not to send her away to protect themselves nor to give her up to the magic-hunters for their own safety. She showed her power trying to save the life of a friend who was attacked by a swarm of bees. She changed herself into a bee and led the swarm away. In the end, she saved her friend and condemned herself.

"Your father went at last when he heard them cry out that their daughter was condemned to be burned to force her to show her true shape as the aur-magic fled her body in death."

Liva shuddered. She would find out who had killed the girl and then she would know who had killed her father.

Liva and her mother struggled together to drag her father's body back home to the cave. Liva tried various different forms of large animals, but in the end, the shape of a hound was the most useful, because it was her mother's form and they could balance her father's weight between them. And so they went, back along the riverbanks, and then through the dense forest.

It took three days, and more than once Liva wondered why they were doing it. Her father was gone. This was only his body. Surely they could bury it where he had died just as well as by the cave.

"He will come home with us. His body will be fuel for the forest around us," said Liva's mother. She held her head straight when she spoke, and her voice cracked as

Liva had never heard it before.

It was dark when they reached the opening to the cave. Liva thought that morning would be soon enough to begin the impossible task of digging in the cold, hard-packed dirt to make a grave for her father.

She crawled into the cave, exhausted. When she awoke, she did not know how much later it was. Her mother was tucked next to her father at the back of the cave, and for a long moment, Liva could almost believe that everything had been a dream, that her father was still alive.

But then it all came back to her. The bear was dead, and her mother was only saying her farewell.

In the morning, Liva and her mother dug the grave together.

Before they covered the body, Liva's mother spoke her last words to the bear: "I always thought I would die before you. A hound is meant to have a short life. Short and filled with adventure and pack. But with you, it was a long life filled with more than I thought possible."

The words were human, or as close to human as they could be in a hound's mouth.

CHAPTER TWELVE
Jens

DAY BY DAY, Jens traveled along the bank of the river up the craggy hills to the densest and most snow-packed part of the forest. The air was thick and wet. He listened to the calls of wolves and wondered whether he would soon think of them as his brothers, or whether they would be as vicious as the boys in his village had always been.

Each day he expected to die, but instead he continued to go, slowly but surely. His leg ached at first, but gradually grew stronger. No animals came near him unless he accidentally came upon them in the dense forest.

The branches overhead were so close together that the sun could only be seen in patches here and there. Jens's eyes became used to semidarkness. He liked that the deep smell of the forest penetrated his coat, his hair, and even his skin.

He ate roots and looked for greens poking out of the

last of the snow. He wanted to survive on those things alone, for he did not wish to kill. But at last he grew too hungry. He determined that if he hunted only to feed his immediate need, and if he killed swiftly, then Liva would not think he had become what she hated.

He began using a knife he fashioned from a sharp stone. When he caught his first snow rabbit, he was so hungry that his hands shook. He could not wait long enough to cook it, and took greedy bites. After the raw feast, he fell immediately asleep.

He woke with a start a little later, and then felt sick at the sticky blood that covered him. He made his way to the river and dipped his head in all the way, then plunged in fully, not bothering to drink, but just using it to scrub himself clean.

When he came out of the water again, though, he was as hungry as he had been before.

After he caught the next rabbit, he made a fire to cook it on, forcing himself to wait as it roasted on a stick. It will taste better, he told himself. But more importantly, it would prove that he was still human.

Satiated, he fell asleep as the fire turned to coals and ash.

In the morning he woke to the sound of snorting.

When he opened his eyes, he found himself staring into the face of a felfrass, its black snout gleaming, its sharp teeth darting in and out of view.

Jens kept very still. This was not Liva. There was no

hint of humanity in those eyes.

The felfrass was smaller than he was, but it was a born predator and could make Jens bleed to death with one blow of its sharp claws or swipe of its mouth. In sleep, he had rolled away from his knife.

Jens tried to pull his hand farther from the felfrass.

It moved one foot forward, then nudged its head closer to Jens's hand and began to lick it.

It was the hand Jens had used to hold the branch over the fire. The meat had sizzled and dripped juices down the branch and onto his hand.

The tongue of the felfrass felt rough on his skin. Jens had to grimace to keep himself from jerking his hand away. What happened if the felfrass rubbed his skin raw and tasted Jens's blood?

But the felfrass became bored soon enough, and sniffed once more at Jens's hand, then turned to the branch itself. Its teeth crunched through the wood as it ate the stringy remains of the hare. When it was finished, it sauntered off without a glance back at Jens.

Jens's vision swirled with black. He steadied himself with a hand and bit back any sound.

As the felfrass disappeared in the distance, Jens got to his feet.

He put his arms around one of the smallest of the large trees and shimmied up its trunk. When he reached the first of the huge branches, he hung over it, his arms dangling, and thought of how many ways he could have died in the night.

Then he climbed several more branches, until he looked up and realized that the tree was so tall, he could not tell how close he was to its top.

His fear was transformed into curiosity.

He climbed branch after branch.

As he got closer to the canopy of the forest, the branches were so close together that he had to push several out of the way before he could move any farther.

He looked down and his vision swam. Now he could see how far up he was, and the world was very small below. His hands clutched tightly to the branches, and he had to breathe deeply to keep himself from fainting.

Then he looked up.

The sun bathed his face, and he could hear insects humming. He could see birds circling overhead. He could feel the sway of the tree with the rhythm of the forest. And he was no longer afraid.

No doubt the felfrass was below him somewhere. And there could be bears and wolves and any number of other creatures who would devour him at a moment's notice, just as he would devour others, in his turn.

There was a hierarchy of life:

Wolves, lynx, bears, hounds, foxes.

Ermines, weasels, martens.

Moose, deer, chamois.

Falcons, kites, ospreys.

Quail, plovers, curlews, gulls.

Beetles, newts, wasps, midges.

Moss, rivers, stones.

He stood in the tree and felt a part of something larger than himself. He reached into his pouch and felt for the two feathers, the snowbird's and the owl's—Liva's. It was a long time before he was ready to descend.

On the ground again, he put his hands to the dirt and ran them through the texture of it, taking pleasure in the feel of bark, bits of bones and teeth, droppings, fibrous roots, and thorns.

He lost himself in the feeling of oneness that had come without any magic at all. He was alone, yet not alone.

When he noticed he was hungry again, he followed the scent of a nearby stream that ran to the river. He waited there as stealthily as he could until he saw a pair of frogs making a meal out of a swarm of dragonflies.

He tried to make himself as small and inconspicuous as possible, crouching down and shuffling forward, his knees close to his chest, his hands in the dirt for balance. He fully expected the frogs to catch sight of him before he put out a hand to grab them.

He had seen boys from the village try to catch frogs before. They had rarely been successful. He had never tried.

But now Jens caught both frogs, one in each hand. One made a low noise, the other simply breathed quietly, and did not try to jump away. Jens killed them quickly.

He went back to the fire pit and stirred up the old

embers, adding more wood. Then he roasted the frogs whole.

How was it possible that he had escaped the felfrass? And that he had so easily hunted with his bare hands? It must be as Liva said: His lack of magic made him invisible.

He could kill as many animals as he wanted to. It was a terrible kind of power.

In the morning Jens tested his theory. He hunted a mole, a hare, and a fox.

Silent, he did not exist to any of them until he held them for death, and then they struggled.

He had only to be speedy, or to set out a trap.

If only he had known it before! He could have gone out hunting alone and brought back a prize that would have astonished the whole village: a bear, a moose, a great buck. He would only have had to kill swiftly and with confidence. Surely that would have been enough to make the village call him a man.

But would that have *made* him a man? He did not think so anymore.

They might have made use of him, but he would not have been one of them.

By the end of his day's experiment, Jens had enough meat to last for a week. He dragged the carcasses back to the fire pit, promising himself that he would not let the meat go unused. He would not kill again until he had to.

He enlarged the fire circle and managed to drag the

log he had cut at several times to sit between the rocks. He lit it and while it smoked, he set up strips of meat to cure.

He scraped the fat off the skins with a sharp stick, then took off his old coat and trousers and wrapped himself in the skin of the moose.

He no longer saw a need to build a shelter. He did not need protection from these animals. If anything, they needed protection from him.

Book Two

The Hunter

CHAPTER THIRTEEN

Jens

IT WAS EARLY spring. After putting the dried meat for the coming week up in the branches of the trees, where animals could not easily get at it, Jens heard human voices on the forest floor below and stopped still. He looked around below and saw three of them, two smaller than the one in the center, who had graying hair and a long, stone hunting knife in his hand.

One of the smaller humans held a struggling polecat. A polecat was not a tasty animal. Even the people in his own village had not grown hungry enough in Jens's memory to eat its gamy, tough meat. But it was one thing to kill an animal for food. It was something else again to torture a frightened creature like this one. It seemed very wrong, and Jens felt a splash of cold anger spread through his body.

He moved down three more branches and listened to the gray-haired man with the knife speak: "The stone in

101

this knife cuts through the animal's aur-magic and makes it flow away." The man held out a knife that looked very much like the one that Jens's father had used before it had broken. It was a layered white stone, touched with gray.

With a swift movement, the man cut into the polecat's abdomen. Jens watched very quietly from the lowest branch as the polecat went still, just as the ram had when his father had used the stone knife on it.

"Do you feel it, Peer, Karl?" asked the older man. "If you close your eyes, you may sense the aur-magic flowing away out of the wound, never to be returned."

The smaller one—Peer?—said, too quickly, "Yes. I can feel it."

Apparently the man did not believe him. He took the knife and held it over the boy's head.

Peer cried out in terror and tried to retreat.

The man grabbed Peer's hand and brought it close to the knife. At the last moment, he let go of the wrist and held only to the smallest finger, twisting it on the blade. Peer went white, and his eyes rolled back in his head. He fell to the ground.

The other boy stepped back from him as if to separate himself from the misdeed.

The man wiped the blood off the knife onto his trousers, then tucked it away, though the hilt was clearly visible. "Never lie to me about the magics. You may think I will not know it, but I always do. A man who is deaf can feel the beat of the music in his bones. A blind man can see another's face with his fingertips. In fact, I believe that I understand the two magics better than those who feel them from within. A man who is trapped in a cage may be the last one who can tell the dimensions of the cage, the material it is made of, and the height from which it is hung from a tree."

"Yes, sir," said Karl, staring at the captive polecat, and then at the fallen boy, Peer.

"Now—what do you feel? Think carefully and only then speak," said the man—the Hunter, Jens thought him, for he had a knife that seemed to cut aur-magic, and he was cold and cruel as in the stories Jens had heard as a child.

Karl was cautious. With open eyes, he held still. Jens was careful that he could not be seen.

"I feel it," said Karl at last. He chewed at his fingernails between words.

The Hunter said, "Tell me what you feel."

Karl looked at Peer, who was still unmoving, and turned back to the Hunter. "I feel the aur-magic flowing away, like a stream."

"Can you press it back into the cat?" asked the Hunter.

Karl hesitated, then made a face of concentration. After a moment he spoke softly, fearfully. "I cannot."

The Hunter nodded. He reached out and touched the boy's head, tousling his long, curling hair. "Good. You speak the truth. Now, think, why should that be the case?

The polecat held the aur-magic once. Is it the aur-magic that has changed or the cat?"

Karl licked his lips. "The cat," he said, more as if it were a question than an answer.

"Are you certain?" asked the Hunter.

Karl looked at the polecat.

"Look into the polecat with your tehr-magic. It is not the same, but it should show you what you need to see."

"The polecat," Karl said again, this time with a little more confidence.

Jens was fascinated by the discussion despite himself. He hated what the Hunter had done to the polecat, but he had never heard anyone speak of the two magics so clearly and openly before. In the village the aur-magic was never spoken of at all without being cursed or spat at. And the tehr-magic was simply expected.

"Tell me," said the Hunter.

"The knife cut into its—shell, you might call it. The part that holds the aur-magic," said Karl. "Because it can't hold it anymore, the aur-magic spills out."

"And what becomes of it?"

"It dissipates."

"It does not become part of the forest magic again?"

"No. I don't know why." Karl had his eyes closed.

The Hunter nodded. "You are right. The knife takes the aur-magic, absorbs it, locks it in."

"So the aur-magic is lost entirely?" said Karl.

"Yes; that is why the knife is so valuable. For thousands

of years humans have thought they were proving their strength against the forest and its animals by changing aur-magic into tehr-magic when they could. But this was only the beginning, the first step away from the connection between animal and human. Do you understand?"

"Yes, sir," said Karl.

"And what will be the final step?" asked the Hunter.

Karl stared at the Hunter a moment. "No magic at all," he said softly.

"Yes. And that is why I had to bring you here. So that you could understand the beginning, the middle, and the end that will come to be. I am the first of those born without any magic, but I will not be the last. The more there are of us, the further we will be from the forests and the animals. We will build greater towns. We will forget the magic entirely. It will be a wonderful day."

"Wonderful," echoed Karl.

Jens's heart clenched. Yes, it was tempting to believe that having no magic made him superior to others. And if one had had the chance to take the magic away from other humans, to make them like he was, he thought there was a time in his life when he might have chosen to do exactly that. But that was before he had met Liva. Before he had seen the snowbird. Before he had come to make the forest his home.

Now he knew that having no magic was an emptiness he would have to live with all his life, but it was not something he would wish on anyone else. He loved the forest and wanted to protect it and its aur-magic. The Hunter, it seemed, had different, more terrifying plans.

If the Hunter's future came to be, then every man would be like Jens's father, with a knife like the Hunter's. How his father had gotten the knife, Jens still did not know. But it had to have been from the Hunter.

The Hunter handed the knife to Karl. "It is the stone in this knife that helps us humans along the path. Some think that a knife made of stone rather than metal is a crude weapon. But it is not so. Try using it yourself. It is easy to use, but it works cleanly, without pressure or strength." He motioned at a plant stalk, and Karl bent over it with the knife.

The stalk split evenly, then began to wilt quickly. It was unnatural, for normally it would take hours before the green would turn to brown.

The Hunter nodded. "What have you learned, then, Karl?"

"That this stone knife destroys the aur-magic of a plant or animal."

"But not a human?" asked the Hunter.

Karl's eyes went wide. "No. It would take the aur-magic from a human as well." It looked to Jens as if Karl did not much like the knife after all.

"And tehr-magic? Would it do the same to it?"

Karl hesitated a moment and licked his lips. "Aur-magic and tehr-magic are but parts of the same thing. Two sides of a coin. Or two states of water, steam and ice. And so, the knife would be as deadly to tehr-magic, I think."

"You see clearly, Karl. This is a great work. We will do it step by step," said the Hunter, holding the knife. "But it begins here."

Jens's legs ached from staying in the same position so long. He wanted desperately to jump from the tree and attack the Hunter. But he had no weapon of his own. He did not fear the magic-killing properties of the knife, but it was still a knife.

He told himself that he would make a plan. He would find a way to defeat the Hunter, to destroy his terrible stone knives, and to protect the forest and the aur-magic.

The polecat twitched once and Jens realized it was not yet dead.

The Hunter let it drop to the ground next to the waking Peer, who started and gasped.

"That could have been you, if I were less forgiving," said the Hunter. "Remember that when we return to Tamberg-on-the-Coast. Remember and tell the others who serve me."

"Thank you," said Peer breathlessly. "Thank you."

As the Hunter and Karl began walking, Peer staggered after them like a blind man being led, touching his wounded finger over and over again, as if that would make it come back to life.

When Jens could hear no more of them, he dropped down from his perch and stood looking at the polecat, which had been left behind.

Its eyes darted this way and that. The Hunter had not cleanly killed it with the stone knife as his father had the ram—whether it was on purpose or not, Jens did not know.

Jens bent over and picked up the polecat as gently as he could, one arm under either part of its body. Jens felt the irregular beat of its heart, directly under his fingertips, the warmth and the shudders of its body. The polecat was white on its belly and around both eyes.

"You can survive," Jens said. "Being without magic, that is. I've been like that all my life." But he knew it was dying.

He petted the cat around one ear, and then the other. He did not know where this polecat's home was, or how to contact another of its kind. He had no way of letting it die in familiar territory.

He was afraid he would have to smother the animal for the sake of mercy. But soon the polecat died without his assistance. Its eyes began to move separately, turning in circles in panic. Jens felt its heart gallop ahead. And then it frothed at the mouth like an animal gone mad.

"I am sorry," said Jens, as he felt the polecat's heart stop.

Jens found himself weeping, for the polecat had been part of his new, true village, and now he felt alone again. He wished he knew how to find Liva, but she was part of his life only in his dreams.

CHAPTER FOURTEEN
Liva

SPRING HAD FULLY come. Liva went out alone in the dusky hours of the morning while her mother slept inside the cave. She intended only to slip out, take in some sharp, fresh air. Since her father's death, she hadn't slept well. Nightmares had begun to plague her, dreams of those with the aur-magic who were being hunted.

That night she had dreamed of a little girl, no more than three years of age, who had enough aur-magic to allow her to change into a bird and fly around her mother's head. The family lived in a remote southern village, and the mother had no idea that the aur-magic was hunted, that it might need to be kept hidden. In Liva's dream a group of men took the family by surprise. They took a knife to the girl that made her scream, and though she lived, she did not change into a bird again. There was nothing familiar in the dream of the girl or her village, and so Liva had no idea how far away she was, but in any case, there was no way she could reach her in time to stop what had already happened.

She wondered how her father had borne the burden of this gift. How often had he dreamed of those who were already beyond his help? Every night? Every week? And how few must have been those he could help. No wonder he had not been able to stay at home. No wonder he had left without a word or a chance to be talked out of it.

Liva took in deep breaths of air, fresh with the scent of rising life. She lifted her arms and let her head fall back. The sky was turning blue, and there were birds flying overhead. Liva could have changed her form to join them, but she wanted to be herself now.

She wore the golden hide of an elk she had killed by herself, at the end of its natural life, and she ran, arms pumping, legs lifting, through the familiar forest.

She had no particular destination in mind. She ran until she could run no more. Then she leaned against a tree to catch her breath. The sound of her blood rushing in her ears was almost as wonderful as the running had been.

She looked around to find that she had run south and was halfway to the human village where Jens lived. Without a storm to slow her, she could go all the way there in a single day. And then what? Walk into the village? She knew she would look wild to them. Though she could speak as they spoke, that did not make her one of them.

And what did she want, anyway? To see Jens again, but she did not want to endanger him. Perhaps she should simply take the form of an animal and pass through his village unnoticed by any but him. Could she be content with that? No, she knew she could not.

She was used to being with animals. She had spent most of her life in the body of one animal or another. But what she wanted from Jens was humanity. Seeing him was not enough. She wanted to talk to him, to feel human with him. She wanted—too much.

Instead of going forward, she turned slowly back toward the cave. She tried to enjoy the rise of the sun, the sweat that trickled down her neck and onto her back. She used her hands and caught a fish. Then she made a fire to cook it, a very human thing. But the fire was too hot, and the fish burned, and the taste of it in her throat made her gag.

Stubbornly she remained human.

She practiced speaking human words, though there was no one to listen to her and understand.

"Good day."

"How are you?"

"I am well. I am human. So are you." She knew that was wrong, though it was what animals said to each other all the time. They agreed they were alike, and sized each other up, then decided whether or not to fight for the territory each wanted. Or they merely acknowledged each other in passing and went on their way.

She tried again.

"Would you like to race me? I can beat you because I am faster and better and stronger."

That did not sound right, either.

"Do you want to touch me? I will let you if you dance for me first. And sing."

Liva shook her head at herself. This was surely wrong for humans.

Then she thought of her mother and father. How had they treated each other? A hound and a bear, but they had been human once.

Liva could not remember much talking between them. They did not share the same language. And though Liva could have translated for them, they had never asked her to. They had become so used to each other, it seemed they never needed to use words to communicate with each other. Her mother had known that her father liked to have his back rubbed at night. Her father had known that her mother wanted to wake late in the morning to quiet.

She could not ask her mother directly, either. It seemed cruel to make her mother face in yet another way all that she had lost. Also, the hound would want to know why Liva was asking, and Liva would have to explain about the human village and when she had been there. Besides, Liva was not sure that her mother knew any better than she did how to be human these days. Her mother had begun as a hound, and though she had lived as a human for many years, she spoke of it as a strain, as if it had never made much sense to her.

And her father—well, he was gone now. Liva's grief was still fresh. He would have teased her about Jens, but she could have borne that. He would have told her stories that would make no sense to her, and then he would have pretended that he had answered everything.

"I know a story," Liva said out loud. "It is about a girl and a boy. Humans. And one day they saw each other and they—"

She swallowed. "They saw each other and they felt as if they had known each other forever. They touched each other and then there were other humans around them, shouting and forcing them apart. They screamed and fought to get free, but they were dragged away and never saw each other again. Still, each night they dreamed of touching again, of a kiss—"

Liva felt warmth spread through her face. She put her hands up to feel it. She did not like the feeling, as if she were ill, but she did not know how to make it go away.

She stopped by the river and sat by the water's edge, leaning back and closing her eyes. She breathed deeply and thought of Jens's face, and the smell of him, and the way he had looked at her.

Then she heard something and looked up in surprised awe to see the snowbird again. All around her the animals stilled, as if to offer themselves to the creature of great magic. But the snowbird flew by without a glance back.

She stared into the blue sky, then tried to change her form to that of a snowbird, which she had never thought to do before. She could not. It was frustrating. She could not remember ever having trouble transforming into any animal before, but her arms changed into an eagle's, though a white one. Her head changed into the shape of a hawk's, and her torso and legs were a black hound's.

She had spent too long being human that day. She had *thought* about being human.

She tried to think of the forest, of magic. She tried another form as a test. With ease she shifted from hound to hare to muskrat to mole, and then from skunk to badger to deer and bear. Then grebe and harrier, tern and dove, ant and earwig and stone fly. She had only to think of any of them, and she changed instantly.

But she thought again of the snowbird—and looked down to find herself half albino bat and half white goose.

The snowbird had almost disappeared. She could see a bit of one wing as it flew over the dense section of the forest in the south. She tried to call it back, at least. But when she opened her mouth, no sound came out, not even the croak of another bird's speech.

The hound, following after Liva yet again, found her there by the river, some time later. "Liva, what is it? You are shaking."

Liva explained about the snowbird, its white wings.

Her mother's response was harsh and cold: "The

snowbirds all died many years ago. It must have been another bird. In the dim light, you were deceived."

"I know what I saw," Liva said, annoyed. "It was a snowbird. What else could it be? Father told me a story about a snowbird. The last of its kind."

"Not every story your father told you was true," said her mother.

"But this one was. I know it was. He told me as if it mattered. But why? What can the snowbird do?"

Her mother refused to meet her eyes. "It is said that the snowbird has a gift of aur-magic for one who fights at the end of time. It should have come for your father. Now it comes too late," she said bitterly.

Liva thought of Jens and of the snowbird's feather in his pouch. Now she had something to tell him about the creature, if only she could find him again.

CHAPTER FIFTEEN

Jens

THERE WAS A wild hound at the bottom of the tree when Jens climbed down one morning. The hound was black but had threads of gray running through her fur. She had a limp on one side, and she looked ferocious.

She stared at Jens, though he had not made a sound, and then bared her teeth. He put up his hands and tried to back away, to show her he meant no harm.

No animal had treated him this way since he had come to the forest. How had she noticed him? More than that, how had she known to track him here? For it seemed she had done that.

She was no ordinary hound.

She was not Liva. She was too old for that, for one thing. And the look in her eyes was not the same as in Liva's, even when she had been a pika.

But the hound had a certain way of holding her head

to the side that reminded him of Liva, and a way of wait-ing. It was not quite animal but not entirely human, either.

Liva's mother? Liva had told him her mother was a hound.

The hound growled low and long, displeased but not threatening. Then she barked sharply and clearly. There were words in her barking, if only Jens could understand them. He had to guess at her meaning.

She barked again.

Jens put his hands out to her.

She sniffed at them, from the tips of his fingers up to his elbows. Then she barked again, with her head held straight out.

"I don't understand," said Jens sadly.

The hound nudged him with her head, pushing him forward.

He did not know which direction she meant him to go in, but he moved. She pressed him harder until he could not walk anymore. And suddenly they were both run-ning, she behind him, making sure that he did not slow down.

Jens was so focused on keeping up the pace she demanded that he did not pay any attention to the for-est around him. He saw only the rocks and the crevices beneath his feet so that he could move around them with-out pulling an ankle. He thought he would collapse and his heart would burst, but at that very moment the hound barked once more and stopped.

Jens slowed down, then turned and looked around. They had come to the foot of a sheer cliff, and the hound pressed him from behind until he put a hand up to a hold in the stone and lifted his feet off the ground. Then the hound continued to bark at him until he had climbed several times his own height and had come to a shelf.

The hound began to call out sharply then, in an urgent tone, and Jens looked around the shelf to see where else he could go. He could not climb higher or even stand up straight. He turned around—and as he did so, his hand brushed against a wooden box covered in leather. Picking it up, he saw that the leather was so old that it crumbled in his hands. He had to look closely at it to see the royal insignia tooled into the top. It was a bear and a hound joined together with a crown over their heads. He did not recognize the coat of arms, but in the north it had been centuries since any kings ruled.

He held out the box, and the hound barked once.

This must be what she had meant him to find, though how she had gotten it up here, he could only guess. Perhaps she had been stronger before? Or had talked another animal or a bird into taking it up for her?

He held the box under his chin, carefully climbed back down the cliff, and handed the box to the hound. Whatever was inside belonged to her. Liva had not said that her mother had been royalty, as well as human, but this made it clear to him. This belonged to her old life.

The hound used her teeth to pull open the box, and there was a flash of light on gold as she held up what was inside. It was a half circlet with a ruby in the center, such as a queen might wear on formal occasions. It showed some sign of scratches, but it was beautiful.

Jens gaped at the hound as she placed the half circlet in his hands.

"But—," he protested. The metal was still warm from her mouth and felt heavy in his hands. "This can't be for me."

The hound barked at him, clearly in the negative.

"For Liva?" Jens asked.

The hound nodded once.

"Why don't you give it to her directly, then?"

The hound stared at him.

"You want me to give it to her?" asked Jens. He felt a moment's bewilderment and then he realized what it meant. A queen never crowned herself. She was given a crown by one who represented the people she was to rule.

"When do I know it is the right time to give it to her?" he asked, looking for the hound once more.

But she was gone.

He put the half circlet in his pouch with the owl feather and the snowbird feather, hoping that he would know the right time when it came.

He felt honored that the hound had chosen him to give the half circlet to. He thought she must have been watching him. Jens did not think Liva had told her mother about him, but if she had, it still meant something that the hound had come to him separately. In the village when a young man was interested in courting a young girl, first he had to make an offering to her mother. In this case it seemed the opposite.

Jens began walking south again, to the huge trees that he had become used to climbing and sleeping in. He heard human voices nearby and pulled himself up to a low branch nearby, then climbed soundlessly higher and looked down.

Karl had returned to the forest. It was perhaps a week or two since he had come with the Hunter, but this time he was with another boy, who shuffled along and had a face swollen with bruises. Whenever the boy slowed down, Karl kicked at him or shoved him down. Jens had been bullied too often in his life not to feel for the victim. But the boy never cried out or begged to be spared. He had a strange dignity, and Jens thought the boy must be used to such treatment.

"You think my father, the Hunter, will reward you for this?" asked the boy, his head raised high enough for him to look straight into Karl's eyes.

Karl slapped the boy's face soundly in reply. "Perhaps he will reward me for it. You have too much magic for his plans, Dofin, and one of these days he will take a knife to you to improve you and make you more like himself. We are all to give up our magic in time, if we are to truly follow him."

Dofin spoke defiantly, his eyes on the ground: "And is that what you want? To give up your magic to him, because he has none of his own?"

"What I want is to show him I am a better heir than you. He will need someone to take his place eventually," said Karl.

Dofin shook his head. "My father does not spend time thinking of his own death, I assure you. He is far too busy planning the deaths of others for that."

"He hates you."

"And I hate him. I hate everything he stands for. You think he has a noble campaign to make humans better and stronger by taking all magic from them? He cares nothing about that. He only wants to make sure no one has a pleasure that he lacks. Do you see how he treats his animals? Kicks them and spits at them and kills them with overwork. It is the same with all those around him. He does not want humans to be higher than animals. He wants everyone to be as low as he feels himself to be, and as alone."

"If you despise him so much, then why do you do everything he tells you to do?" Karl sneered. "You are a coward, or you would leave him. You would let another take your place. But you are afraid. You do not know what you would do without him, who you would be. You take what he gives you because you cannot get any better and you do not care if it costs you your magic in the end."

Dofin gritted his teeth. "I stay because I can best

work against my father when I am closest to him."

"Shall we test your theory?" Karl kicked at Dofin's leg, right behind the kneecap.

The boy went down hard. He did not even try to fight back.

Jens scrambled down through the branches, intending to intervene. He had not fought against the Hunter before because there had been no hope of him winning. But here he could help Dofin, and in doing so, work against the Hunter.

With a piercing sound like a wild hawk on the attack, Jens leaped from the tree and landed to Karl's side. Karl was already spooked at the sound and the sudden fall. But Jens lifted his arms, covered his head in his skins, and then pushed at Karl.

The boy stumbled and fell.

Jens jumped on top of him while keeping his face hidden, and Karl cried out in terror.

Then Jens heard a roar behind him. He turned to see a smallish bear with an intelligent look on its face. He stepped back from Karl, and the bear charged at him.

Karl ran blindly into the forest, the bear behind him.

Jens let the skins fall from his face and looked back to Dofin, who was gaping at the empty spot where the bear and Karl had been.

"Did you call that bear?" he asked. "Did you use your aur-magic to save me?"

"No, that was not aur-magic. I have none."

"But why would a bear chase one and not all of us?" asked Dofin.

"Perhaps the bear wanted a game," said Jens with a smile. "Or perhaps she thought Karl smelled tastier than you or I."

"She?" said Dofin.

"Indeed. That was a female bear. Could you not tell the difference?"

Dofin shook his head. "I am from Tamberg-on-the-Coast. I have never seen a bear before, male or female. You are from a village near here?"

"I have left my village. I live alone in the forest now," said Jens.

Dofin stared up and down at him, apparently believing Jens's story considering his wild and disheveled appearance. "You do not have the aur-magic, yet you live alone with the animals?"

"I do."

"You tame them with the tehr-magic, then. Make them do your bidding."

Jens felt flushed. "No. Certainly not. I would not do it even if I had the tehr-magic, which I do not."

"You have neither magic?"

"Have I not just said so?"

"I am sorry. It is only that I have never met anyone but my father who had no magic at all. And he—he does not live among the animals. He hates them all."

"I am not like your father, the Hunter," said Jens.

"Clearly," said Dofin, nodding. "Well, what reward can I offer you for saving me from that dangerous idiot Karl? Come back to Tamberg-on-the-Coast with me. You can work against my father with me, in secret."

"No," said Jens. It was not that he did not want to work against the Hunter. It was only that he did not wish to do so from within the walls of a town.

"Stay here and safe? You are a coward, then."

"I am the coward? When I live with the animals that you say you wish to save? When I live in the forest you say you will protect from your father?"

Dofin flushed. "If you wish to protect the forest and the animals, you must come with me and work against my father."

"I will do what I choose to do," said Jens.

"Alone?" said Dofin. "You are a fool."

"A fool to whom you owe your life," said Jens.

Dofin lowered his head. "I will give you a reward if you come into town. Coin from my father's treasury."

"What use would those be to me here, in the forest?" Jens said, thinking they would be stolen in any case.

"I must give you something," said Dofin.

"Then go on your way and tell no one about me," said Jens through clenched teeth. "That is surely one gift you can offer me."

"As you wish," said Dofin, and he seemed to bow and step away. But in one swift movement, he had turned back and flung himself behind Jens, grabbing his arms and pushing him to his knees.

Jens did not struggle. "Do you plan to carry me all the way back to the town?" he asked. "I do not think you will get very far."

"I will do whatever it takes to defeat my father," said Dofin, angrily. "And I think that you are necessary for that. You have no magic of your own, but you do not hate it. If I can show to the others in the town that they do not have to be afraid of the forest nor of the aur-magic—I can take away his power. Please," he added grudgingly.

Jens sighed. He found himself admiring Dofin. And yet he still did not want to go back to Tamberg-on-the-Coast with him. It seemed the wrong way to fight one who killed aur-magic, by giving up the forest and all that aur-magic was about.

With one breath, he threw all his weight forward, so that Dofin flipped over his back and landed on the ground, stunned and groaning in pain.

"Coward," he whispered again, lifting his head to meet Jens's eyes.

"I will fight my way. You fight yours," said Jens.

Then the she-bear that had been chasing after Karl came rushing back to the tree. It sniffed the air between the two, then growled and stepped toward Dofin, threatening him with a low rumble.

The bear's claws caught Dofin on one side, but they did not dig deeply into him.

Dofin yelled and retreated, throwing his hands up as

if trying to ward her off. Liva growled once more, and that was all Dofin needed to flee back to the south.

The bear turned back to Jens.

He had never seen Liva like this before, but he was not afraid. "Thank you," he said. It seemed ridiculous that he was standing here, speaking to a bear. But he did not feel he had any right to demand that she should change her form to human. If she wished it, she would have to choose it on her own.

Her face shimmered and shifted. For a moment Jens went absolutely still. Then he saw her bear features change into the fine human features. The small nose he loved, the stark cheekbones, the shining eyes that were the part of her that he could see most clearly, no matter what form she wore.

"Ha!" he said, out of pure joy. "Liva."

She looked down at herself and blushed, and he turned away, offering her one of his outer skins.

"I thought I heard someone who needed help. There was a change in the aur-magic, and I followed it here."

"Oh," said Jens. He wanted to put a hand out to her, to touch her face, to feel the softness of her human skin. But then what? He did not know what to do. The rules of his village did not work here.

Would he offend her if he came too close? Was she interested in him at all?

"I left my village," he said, as though she had not figured that out already. He had to fill the uncomfortable silence somehow. "I didn't belong there anymore. Never did belong there, I think."

"No," she said.

He did not know what to say then. Should he ask her how she liked being a bear? Whether it was better than being a pika? Or an owl?

"I hope you do not mind that I came here," said Jens.

"Why should I mind?" she asked.

Because it was her forest? Because she had everything that he did not?

He sighed. What could he offer her? He put a hand to his pouch but then moved it away. The half circlet her mother had given him was not meant to be used for wooing. And somehow he knew it was not time yet to give it to her.

"The snowbird feather," she said, looking at his hand. "Did you see the bird itself?"

"Yes. I saw it," said Jens.

"I do not think any other humans have seen one," she said. "They are ancient creatures, from the beginning of the world. Most humans believe they have long since died out."

"But there is at least one left," said Jens.

"Yes. It is said that the last of them will have a gift to save the aur-magic. I was born to save the aur-magic as well."

"Yes," said Jens. Was this his conversation with her? Yes, no. Telling her things she already knew. He might as well have been an animal and grunted at her.

"Would you like to hear a story about a mouse?" she asked suddenly.

It was enough to make Jens laugh, so out of place. It was not what he wanted at all. But it was something, at least.

"It is the wrong thing, isn't it?" said Liva. "Of course you do not want to hear a story about a mouse. But it is the only thing I could think of, when I was planning in advance what to say to you."

She had planned what to say to him?

"I don't know humans, you see. I don't know what they do when—" She stopped and colored.

His heart thumped hard in his chest. He was afraid to hope that this meant she thought of him as much as he thought of her. Perhaps he misunderstood.

"I know how animals talk, but I thought I was sure to say the wrong thing to you."

This was so like Jens's own fear that he let out a sound like a laugh.

"I have said the wrong thing, haven't I?"

"No!" Now he was mortified. He should not have laughed at her. Of course that would offend her. He put out his hands. "You don't understand. It's just that I don't—"

She spoke at the same time. "I am not human enough for you, I think. For anyone. I was not sure I wanted to be human before I met you."

Jens stared into her eyes, her human eyes, unlike those of anyone he had ever known. But so perfect. "And now you are?" he asked quietly.

"Yes. I want what I cannot have. I think my mother would say that was the most human thing of all." She twisted her face into a sad smile.

And then Jens saw her hand lift and begin to shimmer into a bear's paw. In a moment she would be gone. He had never felt so many things at once before. In the village he had felt bad most of the time. But when he had felt good, he felt good. Now he felt bad and good and sad and unsure and desperate and hopeful, all at once.

He held out a hand and shouted, "Stop!" As if he had power to stop her from doing anything she wanted with her magic.

She stopped.

"Stay. Please."

To his surprise, she did. And spoke.

"Tell me about the village. About how girls there speak to boys they like to look at."

"You like to look at me?" he asked.

"Why would I not?"

"I like to look at you, too," said Jens. Then he told her about the village, about the traditions of matchmaking, of the dance that a couple did in front of all those who loved them, when they wished to show their intentions toward each other.

"Show me," said Liva, smiling.

Jens showed her the first step, one hand on the small of her back. He could feel the warm pulse of her vein there, and it made him breathless.

"Now what?" she asked.

"Step, step," he got out, stumbling over her.

They tried again, but with the same result.

"I think those traditions are not for us," said Liva, standing to face him.

"I think you are right," said Jens.

"We must make up our own."

But what would they be? It was so much harder when there were no clear signals to show what was meant. To say it all openly was so uncomfortable. It took more courage than anything.

Courage, yes.

"Your mother is a hound," said Jens.

"Yes," said Liva.

"A black hound about this tall." He put his hand to the top of his legs. "With piercing eyes and a sharp bark."

"How did you know . . . ," Liva began. And then she flushed. "She came here, to see you."

Jens nodded.

"She follows me. I am sorry. Did she bother you? Hurt you?" Liva looked him up and down as if for wounds.

"No," said Jens. "It was odd. She seemed to want to get to know me. As well as she could, under the circumstances."

"Truly?" Liva looked suspicious.

"Yes. She was—interesting. She is very proud of you."
Jens thought of the jeweled half circlet.

"She used to try to be more human. With my father,"
said Liva.

"I liked her very much," said Jens. "All humans should
have mothers as protective as hounds, and as persistent."

"She did not tell me she was going to come see you."

"You would have tried to stop her," said Jens.

"Yes."

"You would have had no luck with it, I think. She is
not easily persuaded."

"And she does hate her time to be wasted," said Liva
with a smile. She laughed. "Well, I am glad that you met
her and that she did not frighten you."

"Oh, she frightened me," said Jens. "But in a good
way."

"Do you think I take after her?" asked Liva slyly.

"Yes, very much when you are a she-bear. You are as
fierce and terrible as she was."

"Did I frighten you?"

"Not me, but the other two boys. Isn't that enough?"
asked Jens.

"Well, you knew who I was from the first, didn't you?
You've always known."

"And you always seem to know when to come rescue
me," said Jens.

"I think the last time I came, it put you in danger."

"But how did you know to come this time?" Jens

131

persisted. "You said that you heard someone in the aur-magic call for help?"

"Yes. It was in a dream. My father used to have dreams, too. But then he died. And the dreams came to me. When I wake, I am always in the form of a bear—because the dreams remind me of him." Tears began to fall from her eyes.

He had never seen her cry before. After seeing her as a bear, a pika, and a felfrass, it was strange to see her so human, so soft and vulnerable. "I'm sorry," he said. He should not have mentioned her being a bear. He should have known it would upset her. But he did not know. She had said her father was a bear and her mother was a hound, but he had seen the hound alive. The bear must have died recently, so the wound was very fresh.

"He went to help someone with the aur-magic, but he was killed in a terrible way. Some kind of blade that cuts not just flesh but magic."

Jens pulled back, tension knotting through his shoulders. He thought of the Hunter's knife, and his father's.

Liva did not notice his stiffness. She told him about her father's stories, his games, his jokes.

"You must have loved your father very much," Jens said slowly, and felt a twinge of jealousy, for he had never known such love until now.

"Yes. And now that he is gone, it is all my responsibility. The aur-magic—I must save it. His dreams—now they are mine. I see people at night who are calling out for help."

Jens put his hand to her hair.

She did not flinch away from him, so he stroked the fine dark strands over and over again.

But her body tensed as she spoke: "If ever I find the man who killed my father, I will have my revenge. You should know that. I think I am an animal in that way. Whoever it is, I cannot let him go free. He deserves to die."

"And you think that makes you an animal? It makes you very human, I promise you." Jens had wished for revenge on others more than once: the other boys in the village, even his father.

"It is always life and death when we are together, isn't it?" said Liva, looking up and taking his hand in hers.

"It is," Jens agreed.

"But tiring. Let's do something that is nothing to do with the aur-magic or the end of the world or the snow-bird. Let's just be happy," said Liva. "It's been too long since I was happy."

"I am always happy when I am with you," said Jens. He knew he should tell her about the Hunter's knife, but he was selfish enough to want her attention for himself.

So for a time he let himself forget, and she seemed to forget as well.

He caught a rabbit for her. She caught a fish for him. They ate, and spoke very little, and touched often—yet never enough.

CHAPTER SIXTEEN

Liva

THAT NIGHT IN the forest with Jens, Liva dreamed of a boy with the aur-magic. The boy could not have been more than five years old, with a funny smile, and his front top teeth missing. She saw his parents burning before him. She could not save them, since her dreams only showed her what was happening in the moment, but she had a chance to save him, for he was still alive. For the first time, she was glad she had had a magical dream.

There were images from the dream of a port town that told her he lived south, past the village where Jens had once lived, past the forest where her father had died. Behind the pyre of the boy's parents, she had seen the rise and fall of ocean, and ships in docks. It must be Tamberg-on-the-Coast.

She had heard her father speak of the place, but she had never been herself. There would be many humans there, more than she could imagine. And all of them hated the aur-magic. In her dream Liva saw them shaking fists as the man and woman burned.

It would be dangerous to go there.

The boy was already in custody, captured by a gray-haired man who spoke of hunting down others with the aur-magic. She could not delay. She could understand now why her father's decisions had to be made so hurriedly.

Liva must act quickly, too. She could not stop to wake Jens, nor to return to her cave and tell her mother. She gazed for a moment at Jens's relaxed features, and hoped that she would see him again soon. But he could not help her. She must do this alone.

Liva scratched a message in the dirt, then changed into a kestrel and soared out over the forest. She flew on all day, directly south, following the river. At dark, she could tell by the unfamiliar salty smell in the air that she was approaching the ocean, and the town. Her heart pounded into her throat, and her stomach ached with anticipation of what was to come.

She quested out toward the boy with her aur-magic. She could sense him, but only just.

For her entry in the port town, she debated whether to be a gull or a pigeon, but in the end thought she might try a common magpie, a bird her father had called the least worthy of all birds. He told her mother once it was because a magpie ate the young of other birds.

"And humans do not do the same? And many others?" demanded her mother.

Her father sighed. "Most humans do not eat others of their kind."

"What they do is the same as eating," said her mother.

"You do not like them. I understand," her father said. He turned to Liva. "There was one particular flock of magpies who lived just outside the palace, when we were newly crowned, she and I. They cawed at her, circling, whenever she came out. They smelled the hound on her."

"Horrible things," said her mother.

All those years ago, Liva thought. Her father and mother, king and queen of a kingdom far from here. In some sense, Liva supposed she was a princess because of them, but even the thought of a port town with its many humans frightened her. She had always thought she belonged in the forest.

The sun set brilliantly against the final hill, and Liva smelled the first rank scent of humans gathered together, combined with the salty tang of the sea. She winged closer, using only enough of her magic to feel out where the boy was in the port town. He was on the far end, of course. Nothing could be made easier for her.

She rested for several hours in darkness, and then woke fully and began to plan in the light of the dawn. What shape should she take at this point?

Best to be human, she decided. She'd need to speak to others, to move about and get information. Liva changed herself near a farmhouse where there were a few worn but clean shifts lying out on a fence to dry. She grabbed one, then hurried away. Once she was a safe distance, she put on the rough shift, instead of the soft skins she had left in the forest. Then she ran fingers through her hair, long because it had been some time since she had bothered with cutting it. Her fingernails and toenails were clean, at least. And her teeth.

If she needed anything else to fit in, she would have to get it as she went along.

She took a breath and told herself to be calm, not to assume that she was in danger. She could not, at any cost, change into an animal here, no matter how she was tempted. That would only lead to her being captured and discovered by the Hunter, and that would be no help to the boy.

Keeping her face bent downward, she started into the town itself. Her bare feet were tough and callused, so she felt no pain walking, but the shift was too tight around her chest and chafed under her arms. She did not understand why humans wore such uncomfortable things, but that was the least of her concerns.

Liva walked on the widest street for some distance, few humans awake at that hour to pass by. She went over a small rise and then stopped still at her first sight of the ocean.

It was one thing to smell the water from a distance, to feel it dimly with her magic. It was another thing entirely to have nothing between her and the vast, living thing that was the ocean. She was struck by the caps of white water, the ships lined up along the docks, the gulls cawing up and down the length of the shore. And the life in the ocean itself, calling to her, teeming, moving, breathing.

She gasped as something moved from a rock into the water. A splash came up, and she saw a face. It was almost human, and for a moment she thought of stories her father had told her of mermaids and other half-human creatures that lived in the sea, their magic so strong that they never returned to fully human form.

But then she saw the whiskers on the head and a flash of flippers. A sea lion!

It was a wrench to move from the joy of that feeling to the terror and hopelessness she could sense of the boy from her dream. He was in a small square building near the docks to the south.

The sun was bright now, and Liva could see other humans milling about.

She passed by the boy's building once, then stopped and turned back.

There were metal bars on the windows and guards at the door.

She tried to cross close enough to call out to the boy softly in the language of a gull, which he would surely know if he lived close to the water, but the guards saw her and motioned her away roughly.

She retreated into an alley to watch, then went back when she saw the two guards moving to sit and eat with their backs turned to the jail. Quietly she moved back and put her hands to the wall of the jail. Suddenly a voice cried out behind her, "You there!"

Liva looked behind her and saw two young men. One of them she recognized—she had chased him as a bear in the forest. He had curling hair and fingernails bitten down to the quick. "What are you doing? This is the Hunter's jail. No one should be near it."

"Karl, don't get so angry," the other young man said, hanging back.

The Hunter? Was he the man with graying hair she had seen in her dream, the man who had caused the boy's parents to burn at the stake?

Liva began to move away from the jail. She would have to come back later, sometime when she would not be seen.

"I asked you a question. Who are you?" Karl demanded.

Liva turned and fled.

"Stop! Stop her!" Karl's voice shouted after her.

She could hear the footsteps of the two boys chasing her. They were faster, and they knew the city better. However, they were not running for their lives, and she was.

Liva crossed a cobblestone street and ran down it, heart leaping in her chest as if she were in a hunt. Then she realized she was, but she had never been the one hunted before. She wished she knew the terrain better, and hoped the street did not end abruptly.

Twice figures stood in her way and she slid around them. She had to cross the path of a horse and was able to ask it for help, for it had retained some of its wild speech.

Hampered by the cart it was pulling, the horse did what it could to get in the way of the chasing boys. Liva lifted her skirt and ran still faster. She was not used to running on rock, and the jarring in her spine ran up her back and into her head.

Liva turned a corner, away from the ocean, then turned another corner, back toward it. She thought she had lost the boys behind her, and let herself slow to catch her breath. But as soon as she did, she heard the cry behind her again, "Catch her! For the Hunter! For the Hunter! Catch her!"

If they did not know she had the aur-magic yet, they would soon. She could not let herself be taken.

Yet now she had no idea which way she had come. She had a sense of where the boy in the prison was, behind her, and of where the ocean was, but the rest of the town was a blur.

She ran toward a man who was holding a square frame of wood very gently, as if afraid it would break. There was something strange about it. But before she could tell what it was, she had run into it, and felt the impact of her head as if on stone. She blinked and put a hand to her head, saw blood on it, and felt the warm wetness dripping down her face and into the shift at her neck. She heard the man next to her shouting, "You've broken my glass!" and then there were footsteps coming toward her.

She tried to escape but could do no more than crawl. She felt arms grabbing her from behind, and she used her magic to fight them. It was a mistake.

"She has it! The aur-magic!!" she heard dimly.

But then Liva's vision wavered and the world went dark.

When she woke, her head throbbed and she felt only pain, no magic. It was still early morning, and she was being dragged back toward the boy's jail, away from the ocean.

Liva put a hand to her throat, and felt a necklace around it, with a stone hanging on the end of it. There was something very wrong in the stone—it made it difficult for Liva to breathe. With every step, the stone from the necklace swung out and then hit her in the chest. Each stroke made her light-headed, and more distant from her magic.

She could not get away from it. It pressed on her as if it were a hundred times its true weight. She tried to look into it with her magic, to understand it so that she could break its power. She could see the layers it was made of, each as thin as a leaf, but combined tightly with death.

At last the movement of her captors stopped and Liva saw that she was at the jail again.

"Here she is. Another one for the Hunter," said Karl triumphantly. He pulled her up roughly by one shoulder and thrust her toward the two men who stood as guards, one much younger than the other.

"Nice," said the younger one, staring at Liva, drawing close enough that she could smell the fish on his breath. He moved closer and ran a finger across her jaw.

Liva flinched.

He laughed. "She's a fresh one. Not from here, is she? She doesn't have the look of it."

"What does it matter where she's from? It only matters if she has aur-magic. The Hunter will be pleased with this one," said Karl, swaggering.

"You think this will lift you a notch in his eyes? You think he will ever see you as more than a street boy?"

"I will do whatever it takes. I only have to prove that to him."

"I'll tell him." The older guard looked pitying. "Now, go."

Karl retreated backward through the streets until he had disappeared and Liva was left alone with the guards.

"Like to give me a kiss to make me sweeter?" suggested the young guard in a voice low and thick. He cupped a hand around Liva's head.

But the older guard stepped in front of him.

"You're not to touch her. You know that," he said. Liva could see the sword at his side, but wondered whether he ever needed to use it. His hands seemed just as deadly.

"The Hunter will see to her first."

"I don't see why he cares if we touch her or not. She dies just the same in the fire," said the younger guard.

"If you expect his coin, you follow his rules," said the older guard. He yanked Liva forward.

The younger guard opened the door with a key, and the older guard pressed Liva inside.

It was very dark. She could just see the little boy cowering in the corner. There was an intense smell of fear and human waste.

The older guard nudged her, and she whimpered.

The stone around her neck had smothered her aurmagic and with it her courage. She had never been inside a dwelling like this before. She had slept in a cave with her mother and father at her side, but there had always been an opening at her back, half of one end of the cave. She had always been able to smell the cleanness and the life of the woods beyond.

Here she felt as though she were being buried alive.

She screamed and kicked and thrashed.

The older guard held her firmly. "It goes easier if you don't fight," he told her.

But she tried to call out for help, to anyone nearby, animal or human, to the snowbird she had seen flying overhead. To her mother, to Jens.

Then the younger guard shoved her and she knocked her head again. She felt herself falling, and then tasted the dirt floor against her mouth. There was a click as the door at the front was locked once more.

CHAPTER SEVENTEEN

Jens

JENS WOKE UP just in time to catch sight of the kestrel flying south over his head. He turned and saw that the space where Liva had snuggled next to him was empty.

Where had she gone?

He saw a scratched drawing in the dirt that at first he could not make out. But then he realized it was a map of the path from forest to ocean.

Liva had found out about the Hunter somehow, and she had gone to avenge her father's death. Though he could not go as fast as a kestrel, Jens followed after her frantically, toward Tamberg-on-the-Coast. With every step he had a growing feeling of fear. He had to bring Liva safely back home. He would fight the Hunter or the king or any human or animal that stood between him and Liva.

It was not easy to make his way through the forest.

Because of his lack of magic, he could travel without fear that animals would attack him. But that did not make the trees part for him, or streams dry up, or the day longer. He did not have time to catch food to eat, so he went without. A few berries he found along the way were all that he allowed himself. He did not stop when it was night, but went on. He could only think of Liva facing the Hunter and his stone knife. If she had her aur-magic taken from her, he did not think she would survive the loss.

It was the afternoon of the second day when Jens found himself looking down on the town and the ocean beyond it. He could see no sign of Liva, but he would find her somehow.

He picked his way down the forest path and toward the edge of the town. He walked along, his shoulders hunched around his ears, his every sense confused with new experience. So many sounds, smells, tastes, textures, sights, and colors. So many different faces seeming to blend together.

His clothing was no worse than the clothing of some of the townsfolk he saw. A few were even dirtier than he was and wore shirts with ragged holes.

At a water trough that was close to the center of the town, he saw a woman who looked kind, and old enough to be his mother. "Excuse me," he said.

The woman turned to him. "What's that?" she asked sharply.

It must be obvious to her that he was not from Tamberg-on-the-Coast. "I'm looking for someone," he said. "A friend. A girl. I wondered if you might have seen her."

"A girl from one of the villages in the forest? No. I haven't seen anyone like that, and I wouldn't want to."

"What about the Hunter? Do you know where he is? I want to speak to him. Maybe he has seen her."

The woman's eyes narrowed. "The Hunter would only notice her if she has the aur-magic. Is that what you're saying? You're looking for a girl with the aur-magic?"

"No," said Jens. He had gone about this all wrong.

"Do you have the aur-magic yourself? Perhaps I should call the Hunter's men and tell them. I'll get a fine reward if it is true." She stared at him.

"I don't have the aur-magic," said Jens, wondering if the woman could tell whether he was telling the truth or not.

"Good for you, then."

"The girl is just a friend of mine. I am worried for her because she has never been to town before."

"Then why did she come alone? Girls shouldn't do such things." The woman scowled and moved off.

Jens watched several people come and go at the water trough before he chose another person to approach. This time it was a young boy who looked small for his age and had bright eyes. Jens thought the boy might see more than he told anyone about.

He walked up to the boy. "My name is Jens," he said. The boy said nothing.

"I need your help. I'm looking for a friend who is lost, and I think she may be in danger."

The boy looked him up and down. "She has aur-magic?" he whispered.

Jens took a chance on the boy. He looked around and nodded. "Do you know where she would be if the Hunter caught her?" Jens did not know whether Liva had been caught. She was smart and strong in aur-magic. But she had never been in a town before, and this was where the Hunter had power.

"There is a jail," said the boy. He pointed toward the docks. "It is small, but that is where he holds those he is waiting to burn. There is a public square nearby, where the bonfire is lit."

"Thank you," said Jens. Then he headed toward the docks, the smell of the ocean guiding him. He had reached the dock without finding the jail or the square where a bonfire could be built and was coming back in a circle when he saw Karl.

His cruel face and curly hair were unmistakable.

As soon as he saw him, Jens ducked to the side and hid his face as best he could.

He waited anxiously as Karl passed by, wishing there were trees or bushes around to hide in. When Karl had gone far enough ahead, Jens followed after him. Karl looked to be doing very well. He wore a jacket that had been tailored to him, decorated with gold buttons and trim. He strode with a swagger that had only been developing when Jens had seen him a few days ago. Clearly Karl had earned a recent reward, but whether it had to do with Dofin or with Liva, Jens did not know.

Jens had trouble weaving in and out of the crowds of people. He turned a corner, sure that he had lost Karl. Then he saw him just beyond a large pit in the ground that looked as though it was full of ashes. Jens had to look away.

Karl stopped at a small building, hardly more than a shed, though it was built with thick wood and there were no windows in it. Two adult men stood out front, one younger than the other, but both were well muscled and armed with swords.

This must be the jail.

Karl talked easily with the guards, and Jens held his breath so that he could hear everything Karl said. He laughed about the girl from the forest who had come directly to the jail and then run from it with a speed and uncanniness that proved her aur-magic.

Liva.

Jens waited until Karl had gone. Then he opened his pouch and stared at his possessions. There was only one thing that would be seen as valuable by these men of the town. It was the golden half circlet with the ruby set into it. He knew that the hound had not meant for him to sell it for money, but what else could he do? She would surely not want her daughter to be burned by the Hunter's men, either.

Jens took out the half circlet and closed his pouch.

Then he walked past the guards casually. And then a second time, holding out the half circlet so that it would glint in the late-afternoon sun.

The younger guard turned and stared at it, nudging the other.

Jens stepped forward. "You would like this?" he asked.

"What do you want for it?" asked the younger guard.

The older one shook his head sternly, but the younger one ignored him. "Tell me."

"I want you to open the lock to the jail and let the girl inside go."

"Only the girl?" asked the younger guard.

Jens felt guilty, thinking who else might be inside, and how they would be just as innocent with aur-magic as Liva. But he did not dare trust the guard to let all his prisoners go. One might be let go by mistake. More than that, and there would be no excuses.

"Only the girl," said Jens.

"Give it here," said the guard. "And I'll open the door."

"Open the door first, and then I will give it to you," said Jens.

"Clever, aren't you?" said the guard.

Jens threw the half circlet into the air to let the light shine on it. Then he caught it and looked up. The guards stared. But Jens shrugged and put it back in his pouch. "If you are not interested," he said, and pretended to walk away.

"Wait!" called the guard.

Jens turned back.

"The bauble for the girl."

"Yes," said Jens.

The younger guard took out his key and moved to the lock.

"You're a fool," said the older guard.

"I'll share the coin I get for it. All you have to do is to stay quiet."

"Quiet as the grave," muttered the older guard.

But in a moment the door was open.

"Liva!" Jens called.

She did not come out.

"Don't know what's wrong with her," said the guard. "Must have hit her too hard." He smiled broadly and showed several missing teeth.

"You get nothing unless she comes out." Jens had a terrible feeling. What if they had hurt her? She would have fought with them, turned into any animal shape she could.

The younger guard went into the jail and carried a limp Liva out.

She looked pale, and her eyes were closed, but her chest was moving with breath.

"You see? She's not dead."

Jens nodded, relieved. Then he noticed there was something around her neck. A stone of some kind.

A white stone, like the one on the knife.

Jens's stomach clenched.

He lunged forward, but the younger guard held Liva back. "Throw the bauble to me first," he said.

Jens threw the half circlet as hard as he could, past the edge of the jail into a dark corner.

The younger guard tumbled Liva's body to his companion and ran for his reward.

Jens reached for Liva, but now the older guard held his knife to Liva's throat. "She waits for the Hunter," growled the older guard.

"But—," protested Jens. "I paid you!"

"You paid enough to see her, to know she lives. Not enough for more than that." The younger guard had come back, and the half circlet was nowhere to be seen, except on the smile across his face.

The older guard took the unconscious Liva back into the jail and locked it once more. She would not even know that Jens had come for her.

"No!" shouted Jens. He punched the younger guard's face but was kicked down. The older guard came back and the two worked together to hurt Jens. Dizzy, blood in his mouth, Jens heard voices behind him and realized Karl had come, along with several other boys his age.

But Jens had used the hound's half circlet. It was gone, and he had gotten very little in return for it. He should never have wasted it like that, though he knew he would do it all again, just for the hope of freeing Liva.

"Who is this?" asked Karl of the guards.

"He tried to bribe us," said the younger guard.

"With what?" asked Karl.

The younger guard opened his mouth, then closed it.

Karl reached out his hand. "Give it here," he said.

The younger guard put his hand into his pocket and handed the jeweled half circlet to Karl.

"Pretty. Where would a boy from the forest like you get something like this?" he asked. "Stolen, no doubt, from some old merchant or a wealthy man with ancient heritage." He motioned for the two guards to hold Jens.

"I didn't steal it," Jens said, spitting out blood.

"No? I think you did. Somewhere in the forest where you live, eh? And I am sure the Hunter will wish to talk to you about it, since he fancies himself the ruler of the north. If there are any who think they have a claim to royalty, he will want to know."

"I will tell you where there are more just like it, buried in the forest," Jens said, thinking quickly. "If you let the girl go."

"The girl? The one I caught this morning who turned out to have the aur-magic? You are a friend of hers? Oh-ho!"

"No," said Jens, with a sinking feeling. "Please. I only want to help the girl."

It was no use. Karl called for rope, and Jens was soon bound with his hands behind his back and his feet tied together.

Jens told himself to be calm as they dragged him

away from the jail, toward the ocean. He might still do something for Liva. If he could talk to the Hunter, convince him of—something. He would not give up.

By dark, Jens was tied to a post and left alone. The smell of salt and death was all around him, and he could hear the lap of water near him. Soon he could also hear squeaking and scratching.

Rats.

He could not see them, but he could feel them coming closer. And then he remembered that rats were wild animals, with aur-magic.

Jens held himself absolutely still, trying not to breathe any more than he had to, keeping his legs from twitching no matter how much they hurt.

And the rats stopped.

They moved around him. He could hear their scurrying little feet, could even hear them dragging meat back with them—and the smell of it, always rank. The remains of a fish that had been left out for several days. Or a dead cat or dog, Jens suspected. But the rats did not sense him. As in the forest, if he made no sound, they did not notice him, because he lacked all magic, and magic was the way they sensed the world around them.

CHAPTER EIGHTEEN

Liva

W HEN LIVA AWOKE, it was to a terrible
pain in her head and a deadening feeling
around her throat. The only light came
from the cracks in the roof and in the doorway. It was not
much, but it was enough to see that the boy was still there
with her, in the corner far from the door.

"Hello?" she said, the human language strange in her
ears.

The boy did not answer.

Liva struggled with the stone necklace, trying to turn
her head this way and that to get it to fall off. But that did
not work. At last she forced herself to touch it. It burned,
but she threw it off with a supreme effort of will. She did
not think that anyone who had less magic than she could
have thought of how to fight against it. But at the sound
of it dropping to the floor, she breathed relief. Then she
moved away from it and slowly toward the boy.

He pulled himself upright, flattening his back against the wall.

"I have magic," she said. She tried to give some to him, but what did not seep out of his wounds, he pressed back at her, as if afraid to take it in.

"Can you speak?" she asked.

He began to breathe more quickly, as though the very sound of another human voice frightened him.

Probing the boy's magic, Liva found it was cut in several places: on one leg, across a wrist, and in dots over his chest. But he would live.

"Do you have a name?" Liva asked, as a beginning. "I am Liva." When he looked up at her, she said her own name again, and pointed to her chest.

The boy looked away again a moment later, but then he moved an inch closer to her.

"Tern," he whispered.

"Tern," Liva echoed.

Beckoning her closer, he used his magic to change his hand from a sturgeon's fin to a tern's wing to a lynx's paw, and then back to a human hand again.

Liva put out her own hand and did the same simple sequences of changes.

Tern did the sequence over and over again. At last, Liva realized he was doing it to show her what was wrong with him, not what was right. Whatever had damaged him had made it so that he could not change his whole body, only his left hand and part of his forearm.

155

"I understand," said Liva.

He kept doing it.

Liva thought he must have learned the sequence from his mother or father. Now they were gone, and this was all he had left of them.

There was a scraping at the lock of the door.

Liva scrambled with her hands to reach for the stone necklace again. She hated how weak it made her feel, but she did not want her captors to know she could remove it, so she put it back around her neck.

Tern made a soft sound of distress. He curled up in himself, and put his head to his chest, as though that would make him disappear.

Liva turned to face the person at the door, the necklace swinging around her neck to land on her chest with a burning sensation. A flash of light blinded her for a moment, but she blinked and saw a man, tall and strong, with keenly intelligent eyes and a cruel look. His hair was gray and tied neatly back, his clothes finely cut, and his nails were carefully clipped and clean.

Liva felt her legs spasm, as if they were trying to run away. She knew him from her dream, but in person he was worse.

There was something dangerous about him. Not wild, but fierce and unpredictable.

He looked over Liva and the boy, and gave a chilling, wide smile as he closed the door. Only cracks of light from the wood now showed where he stood.

156

"Ah, my young friends have done their work today. They will be well rewarded indeed," said the man.

This was the Hunter. Whatever had been done to the boy, he had had a part in it. And since it was very similar to what had been done to her father, Liva felt queasily that perhaps she had also found the man she had wanted vengeance against. But here she was, in jail, with no way of striking at him, her aur-magic damped by the stone necklace, and with responsibility to the boy foremost in her mind.

She had to save him first.

The Hunter stepped forward, and the boy began to sob.

Liva moved between them.

The Hunter reached for her arm and pulled her to him. "Tell me where you are from and how many others like you are there," he said, twisting her arm until she was afraid that he would wrench it out of its socket entirely.

Liva held her lips tightly together and began counting to ten in every animal language she could think of. Anything to keep her mind occupied with something other than fear.

Then she saw the Hunter take a stone knife out of his belt.

Her mind went on, counting in the language of the dovekie, but she could feel the tremors beginning in her eyes and moving to her lips, her cheek, her neck, and downward.

Without a word, the Hunter lunged toward her and sliced with the knife at Liva's stomach. A shallow cut, but Liva gasped and began to weep. The stone knife had left a hole in her magic. What had been there once was now gone. Suddenly she knew for certain: This was what had been done to her father, a thousand times over.

The emptiness left behind was worse than pain. Liva wished the Hunter had cut off her arm instead, or taken one of her eyes. She was sick at the thought of how her father must have felt as all sense of magic was taken from him. Liva would always remember what the Hunter's knife had taken from her.

It was the language of an owl, including the mating call she had always loved.

"And now." The Hunter held out the knife toward the boy.

Even without being touched by it, Tern fell forward, his whole body shivering, his hands behind his back as if they were being held there.

The Hunter seemed to be enjoying the moment. Certainly he was in no hurry.

He moved forward slowly.

Liva took a breath, gathered her strength, and threw herself against his back. There was a satisfying sound of his exhalation of air.

Then she fell to the side, rolled, and hit the wall.

She moved gingerly away.

The Hunter got up, brushing himself off. "Well. You've

come after him, have you? One of the aur-magic family, eh? A younger cousin, poor, helpless, weak. And you put yourself in danger to save him. Foolish girl. You are hardly older than he is. And you have no defenses against me."

He lifted the knife again and moved toward Liva.

"Take my aur-magic then," she said. "But let him go." She nodded to Tern. "You have no use for him now."

"Ah, not true. He has aur-magic still," said the Hunter.

"He is no threat to you or anyone in this town. He can't use his aur-magic now for anything that matters," she said.

"Anything that matters to you, perhaps. But it is aur-magic for all that, and it is wrong."

"What is wrong with having aur-magic, then?" asked Liva.

"The aur-magic is the way that we are bound to animals and to their world. We will never rise above that beginning so long as we still have aur-magic to remind us of that baser side of ourselves." He made a fist and slammed it into the open palm of his other hand. "Humans are not animals!"

Liva stared at him, aware that at that moment he looked more like an animal than any human she had ever seen before, and in the worst possible way. A snarling wolf, in fact, long starved from winter, and eager to attack the first creature it found, no matter what its chances of survival.

The Hunter grimaced and seemed to consciously make a decision to drop his hands to his sides. He spoke softly. "If we are to grow past what we once were, we must destroy what belongs in the past and move on to the future."

"I do not believe I want your future," said Liva steadily.

"That is only because you are still caught so much in the past," said the Hunter. "You have spent all your life as an animal in your aur-magic. But now it is time for you to be human, and this knife will help you become like I am."

"As you have helped him?" asked Liva, staring at Tern.

"Indeed, as I have helped him. Though burning would perhaps help both of you more." Then the Hunter knocked on the door, and there was a sound of jingling keys.

"Just as a warning," said the Hunter casually, not even turning to speak to her directly, "if you escape from this place, I will not only see the boy burned, but I will make sure that he suffers terribly first. I will take the rest of his aur-magic slowly and cruelly. And he will call for you to help him, so that you will feel his death on your heart for the rest of your days."

For all her attempts at disguising herself, Liva knew she had shown too much strength, even with the necklace around her. No doubt anyone else wearing it would have been unable to resist in any way, and she had done so at every possible turn. She had not thought of the price she would pay for it. Perhaps the Hunter was right. She was used to dealing with animals, and in a battle with an animal, there was no subterfuge. It was only a matter of which was larger and faster and fiercer.

But animals did not take hostages, either.

CHAPTER NINETEEN

Jens

ENS'S HANDS WERE ragged and bleeding from pulling on the ropes, and his feet were numb with pressure when he heard a group of men coming toward him. His blindfold was torn off, and Jens had time to register that it was still dark, but then he found himself looking into the face of the Hunter.

"Karl told me that you tried to help the girl in the jail escape. You bribed the guards with a very valuable item." The Hunter held up the jeweled half circlet and tossed it back and forth from hand to hand as if it were no more than an ordinary seashell. "Tell me about her and I will give this back," he offered.

"Why do you want to know about her?" Jens asked. "Are you afraid of her power?" He did everything he could not to sound frightened. Liva was still alive, and that was good. But he did not want to give any information to the Hunter that might harm her. He certainly did not believe that the Hunter would give him the half circlet, or anything else he promised.

The Hunter put away the half circlet and took out his stone knife. "She has a good measure of the aur-magic, I will admit. But I have this stone knife to cut into her. I will cut into her again and again, if necessary. And if that stone breaks on her, I will get another. And another. I assure you, she will not escape me. No, I am not afraid of her power. I am merely curious about how she has eluded me for so long. And I think you may have some answers."

Jens thought of the bear and the hound and how they had protected their daughter, taking her so far to the north, making sure she had no contact with humans. He shook his head. "I don't know anything about her," he lied.

With a shrug, the Hunter took the knife and put the point of it at the base of Jens's left eye. "Tell me her name," he said. "Only her name. That is all I ask. It is such a small thing, to save your eye, is it not?"

"Whose name?" asked Jens, and he kept his voice steady. He kept his body proudly steady, too, though the knife cut into his face and the blood dripped down his chin. But the Hunter leaned closer to him and stared at the wound.

Jens realized in that moment that he should have pretended that magic was pouring out of him. The Hunter expected it from everyone else.

"The rats did not touch you. The knife cuts only your body. You have no magic at all," the Hunter said, his voice half in awe. "I have been waiting to find another born like myself—"

He leaned in closer to Jens and touched lightly on Jens's naked chest. Jens felt as if there were tiny pinpricks in a pattern around his heart. "No, not born this way, after all," he said. He paused a long moment, and Jens pressed himself to silence, despite his curiosity. Then the Hunter shook a finger.

"We met once, years ago," he said. "You may not remember me, but I remember you. I was impatient with waiting to find others without magic. I knew that they must be born somewhere, but perhaps too far from here. And so I began to make others without magic on my own, so that I could see how they grew.

"Many times I have wondered if I would come across you again. I should have known the first moment I touched you. I remember it all so very clearly." The Hunter let out a breath slowly, and his face looked as if he was in ecstasy.

The hairs on the back of Jens's neck rose.

"You look like her, you know, especially around the lips. She had such beautiful, pale, pouting lips. Has anyone ever told you that about your mother?"

Jens went cold. It was not possible that the Hunter had known his mother. She had died so long ago.

But the Hunter went on speaking. "Would you like to

164

hear of her death? I suppose you must have heard some tale or other as you were growing up, but your father would have withheld the whole truth from you. He likely did not want to remember it himself. But the other villagers, they knew some of it. Did they treat you badly as a child? Did they make sure you knew you were damaged? Your mother had the aur-magic, though her village did not know of it. That is why I must constantly patrol all villages too close to forests, because those within them are far more likely to have the worst of the magics."

Jens did not answer. He would not give any sign that he believed the Hunter, not one.

"She had hair as pale as yours, though cleaner and better kept. She always wore it in braids circled above her head. She was tall and lean, her hands rough with work. She did not even try to hide her aur-magic. She seemed to love doves above all other animals. She would make little figures of doves, with absurdly wide white wings, and set them to fly around the village.

"Your father found her aur-magic attractive. He loved her too much—enough even to let her bear a son who would have the same aur-magic that his mother did."

What? Jens had never had magic.

"I came to the town and saw that she was near birth. I waited until the time had come upon her. Your father had gone out hunting, you see, to make sure he had meat when she needed to rebuild her strength. And the other women in the village went to get water for her. But when

165

they saw me, they did not stop me. They kept away as I approached her hut."

No, Jens's mind screamed.

"I came to the door and had only to put my knife against it before it parted for me. She lay on the floor, wrapped in wool blankets, and next to her was a small, squalling red face. There were still streaks of salty sweat lining her face from the effort of birth. Her husband was not with her, and she would have done anything to draw me from her child. She thought to save you from my stone knife, to protect you and your aur-magic, and to make sure that the world still had the gift of her ancestors."

All Jens's life, the villagers had told of how his mother had died because of him, and how he had lain with her body for three days until his father returned from a hunting trip and found them both.

And all this time, Jens had felt guilty for his mother's death. But it had nothing to do with him. She had not died because of him. She might never have died—if not for the Hunter.

"She saw me and she got to her feet with great effort," the Hunter went on, his eyes distant. "I think she believed her aur-magic would disguise you.

"She stood in front of you. 'And so you have come for me,' she said.

"'You must consider it a compliment, for I do not bother with those who are unimportant,' I said to her.

"She did not answer me, but tried to push aur-magic at me to throw me off balance, or perhaps even to kill me.

166

I think she was not so stupid, though, as to think it would work.

"I held up the knife, and it cut to pieces the aur-magic she tried to press toward me. Then I took the blade to her flesh. The magic dripped out of her, but she did not cry out in terror or pain. Instead she looked at me with pity.

"'I know what you are,' she said. 'I have felt the horror in you. Let me give you magic to heal you.'

"As if I needed her! I was angry at her superiority. So it always is with those who have the aur-magic. They think it is their right to rule over us, to be kind to us, to condescend and share their largesse with us. Well, I taught her the truth of the matter. Magic is nothing. And so I prove, day by day.

"She died as I cut her again and again. I think it was her love for you that kept her alive for so much longer than the others. For your sake, she tried to live."

Jens did not want to hear more. It was too horrific. And yet, his mother had died trying to save him. That part was something to hold to his heart. She had not died for hatred at the sight of him, as his father had sometimes told him cruelly.

"When she was dead, I turned to you. Quiet there, though your eyes were open. Your hand was in your mouth. Not just the thumb of it, but the whole fist, and you made a strong sucking sound, but no cry.

"I took off the great wool blanket she had put you in, as if you were a bear cub instead of a human baby. I took

167

the knife to you and I cut tiny slivers into your skin, all over your whole body, so small that they left neither blood nor scars, but enough so that you could hold no magic of either kind."

Jens had to hold his head straight ahead to keep himself from looking down for signs of the Hunter's knife, all those years ago.

"Then I left you there, still living, but with your magic gone. And now you have come back to me, to show me the results of my handiwork. I worried you would not live long. But now I know why this old blade cuts only into your body. It has already done its work on your magic, more thoroughly than any other that has ever felt the knife and lived.

"You are my masterpiece, and you did not even know." The Hunter let his hand slide onto Jens's spine, and then gave a cry of joy.

"It is almost enough to make me set you free. But not quite. For I think I could use one such as you here. And you owe me. Your life, such as it is, has always been mine."

Chapter Twenty

Liva

IT WAS SOME hours later, nighttime. Liva heard the sound of loud, drunken singing coming from the guards on the other side of the locked door of the prison. She had been rubbing Tern's back until he fell asleep. Now as she slipped him off her lap, he murmured, "Mama." She was determined that his trust would not be in vain. Her father had died and she had not saved him, but Tern she would not sacrifice. Not for anything.

Liva had taken the stone necklace off earlier and set it as far from her as she could, while being able to still reach it at the sound of the door.

There was laughter and then a key turned in the lock. Sensing with her magic, Liva was sure the Hunter was not behind the door this time. It was only the guards. But what did they want?

Liva crept toward the door and crouched. Her

aur-magic, this close to the nearby necklace, was too weak for her to transform herself fully, but she changed both of her arms into those of a bear.

When the door swung inward, she slammed into it with the strength of her bear's arms. There was a sound of grunting surprise, and then a stifled cry of pain.

She stepped through the door.

The two guards were struggling to find their feet. At the sight of Liva's rapier-sharp bear claws, the younger one gave up and scrambled backward before turning tail and fleeing. The older one stood and held out a sword.

Liva flung one of her bear arms at him and caught him by the shoulder. His shirt opened and his skin burst. Blood splattered her. He fell down after a long moment with a sigh. Liva could see the rise and fall of his chest, so he was not dead, but he would not be rising soon.

Liva wished she had been able to get the other guard as well. Now she and Tern had to move quickly. If the other guard had gone to tell the Hunter what had happened, the Hunter would be after them both soon.

Changing her bear paws back into human hands, she looked up behind the town to the hill into the forest, thinking about the difficulties in getting Tern there. It was already dark, and it would take hours to reach that far with the young boy at her side. She could not transform into any animal to carry him, because that would reveal them both more surely than the Hunter's call.

"Tern, come," said Liva, going back inside the jail.

The boy stumbled to his feet, blinking his eyes rapidly. Liva thought for a moment he would sink back into the stupor of the jail, but he nodded, and a look of determination spread across his face. He stepped out and looked at the fallen, bloody guard.

"Follow me," said Liva, to distract him from the sight.

"That one tied Mama's hands." Tern rubbed his wrists, and Liva guessed that he was remembering his mother being led to the bonfire where she was burned.

"Well, now he is hurt, too," said Liva.

Liva took his hand and he did not fight against her as she pulled him into the shadows. She forced herself not to run, to walk at what would appear to be a leisurely pace.

The first thing Liva did was get both of them away from the jail. She did not care which direction she went, but took the first street she found and turned away, and did it again when she came to the next street. She made up a story in her head about herself and Tern. He was her younger brother. She was bringing him home to their parents. They had played long and hard that day and were very tired. He had gotten lost, and Liva had spent hours finding him. She might be a little sharp with him, in exhaustion.

When she saw a couple staring at them, she scowled at Tern. "Home," she said. "We have to get home or we'll be in trouble with Mama and Papa. Hurry up, you." She didn't dare use his real name, in case the Hunter had made it well known.

"Mama? Papa?" said Tern, his face suddenly light, and his stumbling legs sprightly and deft.

"Yes," said Liva, hating herself.

As soon as she got away from the couple, she had to tell Tern the truth. "It was a story," she said. "About a different mama and papa. Not yours. You know already where they are, don't you?"

Tern sighed and slumped forward. "Fire," he said.

"Yes. But what remained of their aur-magic returned to the air and the forest. Take comfort in that. For we are going to the forest."

"Forest," said Tern.

Liva did not say anything about her story aloud again. They walked as it grew dark. There were few people left on the streets by then, except for those who slept there. Liva was afraid every moment, not just because of the Hunter's men who might come for them, but also for the other dangers of Tamberg-on-the-Coast. A port town would have many layers of criminals, and the Hunter was only at the top. She and Tern could be attacked by any number of those, and if Liva used her aur-magic as protection, it might only make things worse.

Close to dawn she had to stop, for Tern was dragging himself along and breathing so heavily that he had become conspicuous. She searched for a safe place to hide for a while, a tree or a bush. But there were none in the town.

172

She chose a pile of refuse that stank and swayed in the slight breeze, but she thought that she and Tern could pass as street children themselves now. Better if others were afraid of them than the other way around.

"A moment," whispered Liva to Tern. "We'll rest for just a moment."

She let herself take several deep breaths.

"Forest?" said Tern.

"No, not yet," said Liva.

"Mama, Papa?" asked Tern.

"No," said Liva, her heart heavy.

"Home?"

"Soon," said Liva.

He tucked himself next to her and was sleeping in moments.

Liva watched as the town gradually came to life over the next hour. When it was fully light, Liva knew it was time to move again. She hated to wake Tern, though. He needed sleep, and she felt guilty already for all that he had suffered before she had come to help him.

Liva looked around the growing stream of people moving into the center of the town, toward the ocean. It was then that she saw the old woman pushing a cart. She wore a scarf wrapped around her face and she moved with a lurching, stumbling gait. The woman's aur-magic was small, just curling around the edges of her heart.

Liva had gone longer periods than this without food; she might have passed the woman by and tried to go on alone. But Tern had been in the jail for much longer than Liva, and from what she had seen, he had been offered very little food during his stay there. And the Hunter had weakened him in more ways than one.

So Liva approached the woman. "Please," Liva said, standing in the woman's way. "My brother is very weak with hunger. We are trying to follow our parents, but they have gone ahead." She gestured vaguely to the north. "Can you help us?"

The woman wore no smile, but she was sturdily built, and her face was softly wrinkled. Liva thought she looked like an owl, and liked her even more when she pressed her lips into a circle and let out a low hoot.

"You're aur-magic. Both of you. Ain't you?" she said. "It's in your faces, in your sadness and in your desperation."

Liva tensed. She could not harm this old woman, but she must be prepared to flee. "Now, don't worry none. I'm not one of the Hunter's. I won't betray you. Is he chasing you?" She looked around them, and Liva did the same, but as yet the morning was cool and very quiet.

"Not yet, then. I expect the dogs will come out before long."

That thought sent a chill through Liva's heart.

"But I won't let him have you."

Tern stirred. "Mama?" he said to the old woman.

"No," said Liva again, her heart breaking.

But the old woman put an arm around him and kissed

him on the cheek. Tern seemed to rest more easily then.

"I'm sorry. He's confused," said Liva.

"Nothing to be sorry about. I take it as a compliment when a child wants me as a mother. Never had enough children of my own to satisfy me." She struggled to put Tern's sleepy form into the cart, but Liva helped her, and together they managed to get him in without banging his head or limbs against the hard, wooden sides.

"We can push it together," said the old woman. "We'll cover him with some blankets and it will look natural-like."

Liva said nothing about the jail or about Tern already being captured and tortured, but the woman seemed to have guessed it already. Hoping she was doing the right thing, Liva did as the woman said. They began walking.

"You need to get north, I daresay. To the hills and the forest beyond."

"Yes," said Liva.

"Well, we'll see how far we can get you." The woman gave her a bit of hard bread that crumbled as soon as Liva touched it to her mouth. It was salty and dry and tasteless. But it settled her stomach. Tern seemed to like it as well.

Liva began to think the woman was too good to be true. Could she be a spy of the Hunter's, taking them back to him? She looked suspiciously at the woman, who read her gaze.

"You think that everyone in Tamberg-on-the-Coast is

175

like the Hunter?" asked the woman.

Liva did not know how to answer.

"It isn't so," she said. "Some of us hate him. Him and his burning and his speeches against magic. We know what's what. We know what the aur-magic is to all of us, and how it keeps us alive. We know how there is no tehr-magic without the aur-magic, too."

"Then why do you let him have power?" asked Liva.

"He took it before we knew what he was doing. In order for us to fight him now, many of us would die. He has the strength, but that does not mean he will always have it. We wait. One day his own men may rise up against him. He does not treat them well. And when that happens, we will be free again."

The woman offered her dried berries. They were very tart, a variety Liva had never tasted before. "Gor berries," said the woman. "Growed in my own yard, by my own hands."

A long, low whistle came from the distance. The woman started, and Liva knew what this meant. She and Tern had been discovered gone.

As soon as the whistle stopped, there was the call of barking dogs. They barked in imitation of human sound, and it pained Liva's aur-magic. Of all the animals, the wild hounds were those she knew the best. The language of the wild hounds was like a mother's lullaby to her ears. This—it felt like claws to her heart. This was aur-magic twisted into something else.

"You must get gone and quick, both of you." The woman reached into the cart and pulled off the blanket that had covered Tern. She shook him awake and tried to help him climb out. He was confused and clumsy.

Liva had to lift him.

"This is as far as I go," said the woman.

Liva nodded, holding Tern. "You have helped us enough. Thank you. I do not blame you for not giving us more."

"You do not blame me, but I do. To think that we were ever taken in by him and his promises—we thought he would tame the forests by killing the magics, and bring us easy living. We did not see the price of it."

Liva put her hand on the woman's arm and squeezed. "Go now," she said.

"And you," said the woman.

Tern began to sob tearlessly, and she could feel the shaking of his ribs against her own chest.

"She has to go," Liva whispered in his ear. "She is trying to save you." Steeling herself against the sadness, she carried Tern down the street and found a shed to hide him in.

"Remember," Liva said. "We are going home to the forest. Where the aur-magic lives." She held Tern's eyes and used her magic to make him sleep. Then she went out to meet the Hunter and the dogs. It was the first bright light of morning by then, and the sun was at her back.

The Hunter squinted in the light. He had one human

at his side—Karl. In front of them stood four huge dogs, nearly as tall as any human. Liva was surprised he had not brought more men with him. It showed how little threat he thought she was to him, after all.

Well, she would show him.

Liva ran at the first dog. It snarled and snapped at her, and Liva could smell its rank breath when its teeth came close to her face. She changed then into a bear fully, for she had no more reason to hide her aur-magic, and stood up on her hind legs, roaring.

The dog whined and fell back.

Liva challenged the other dogs with another roar.

Then the Hunter stepped out into the street and called the dogs back to his side.

As a bear, Liva felt confidence. Her father had not had her aur-magic when he faced the Hunter. But she was ready now. Or if she was not, then she never would be.

"I thought you might have rejected my first gift because it was too small. So I brought you this one instead," said the Hunter. He had a huge stone, the size of his own head. He threw it toward her, and it rolled to a stop at her feet. Before she could move away, Liva felt her magic drained away by it.

Liva felt her body lose the shape of a bear, and she was quickly on her knees, her head on the ground, hardly able to breathe. She tried to tell herself that she had the aur-magic still, though it felt completely lost. She only had to get away from this stone.

But she knew that the Hunter would have his knife. He planned to cut her. It was only a matter of time.

"Where is the boy?" asked the Hunter.

Liva shook her head weakly.

"Oh, I will find him. But first I will deal with you. I am so glad to discover you have even more aur-magic than I thought. I have been looking for a challenge. There was a man-bear not long ago, but—he was not as difficult to kill as I had hoped." The Hunter's eyes met hers.

She lurched to her feet and threw herself at the Hunter. She had little strength left beyond that of a normal human, but what she had, she used to some effect. She scrabbled at him with her frail human fingernails, leaving scratches down his face and side. She spat at him and punched at him until he pushed her away from him and laughed.

"Is that all?" he said. "I would have thought it would be more. Your friend thought that you would defeat me."

Her friend? Liva went very still. She had only one friend. Jens. But she had left him in the forest, safe. Why had he come after her?

"A handsome young man," the Hunter went on. "I can see why you are so close to him. He is the only human who would have you, is he? The others are all too afraid of your aur-magic. But he can't sense a bit of it. And he's half animal himself."

Liva spat at the Hunter and tried to reach him again with her hands, but he slapped her down. At least Tern was hidden, she thought. She clung to that hope.

"Don't think I won't find that little boy. I will search the whole of Tamberg-on-the-Coast. He will not thank you for making him believe that he could get away from me," said the Hunter.

Dimly Liva heard the sound of another bark, coming from a distance. It did not strike her that this hound spoke in the language of wild hounds until she saw her mother's black form streak past her.

"Go!" Liva's mother barked at Liva.

"But—," she protested.

"Go now! Obey me and live!" her mother commanded.

The stone made it very difficult for Liva to move.

She watched as her mother leaped at the Hunter's throat and pushed him back. There were marks on his chest, and his head banged into the stones of the street hard. He spat up a little blood. But then the dogs began to attack the hound, and the Hunter had a chance to gather himself.

Her mother was lame but fought fiercely, and Liva wondered whether the white stone affected her the way it did Liva. Yet the hound would not retreat.

The Hunter called back the dogs when Liva's mother had fallen and did not try to get up.

He kicked her in the abdomen, and she made a terrible, soft sound.

With a huge effort, Liva crawled forward and put a hand to her mother's face. The eyes were still open, the gaze steady. Her mother coughed, her body wracked with the movement.

"Told you," she whispered. "Go." She bared her teeth and snapped them, as if to nip at Liva.

Despite all, Liva smiled briefly. This was her mother, protecting her daughter to the end.

The Hunter kicked the stone, and it came rolling closer to Liva until it touched her on one side. She went numb there: arm, leg, chest, face. It was as if the Hunter had cut her in half, and he had not even taken out his knife.

The Hunter sneered at her, but he turned toward the hound.

"Please," Liva begged. "Please!"

Her mother called to her, in the language of the wild hounds, "My daughter!"

The Hunter laughed.

He took out his stone knife and plunged it into the heart of the hound.

Liva felt her mother's death like a burning sensation. It was worse than the feeling of the white stone that stole her magic. This stole something deeper in her.

Suddenly there was a shadow over her, and Liva looked up. "Snowbird," she murmured.

The Hunter followed Liva's gaze. "What is that?" he demanded.

"Can you not feel its aur-magic?" Liva asked weakly. "More than mine. More than anyone's you have ever seen." Liva had not meant it as a challenge. It had been pure awe speaking.

But now the Hunter was incensed, his eyes bright and angry. "I will get it," he said. "I will conquer its aurmagic. And then there will be none left."

He ran, leaving Liva behind, chasing after the snowbird, calling at the top of his lungs for his men to get out their bows and stone-tipped arrows and begin shooting.

Liva was afraid for the snowbird but was not in a position to help it. Surely not even the Hunter could do anything against a power so elemental and enormous as that one.

Her heart torn with grief, she turned back to her mother's body, but Karl was approaching rapidly. Liva remembered what her mother had told her. She had to run.

She tried to change into a wolf, but she could only get her right half to change, and there was no use in half a wolf's body. She thought of Tern, who could only change his hand. Had she become like him, or was there still hope that she might recover from the touch of the stone?

For now all that mattered was getting Tern and getting away from here. Later she could think. Later she could plan what to do to help Jens, to stop the Hunter. Later she could regain her strength.

CHAPTER TWENTY-ONE

Jens

*J*ENS SLEPT FITFULLY during the night, dreaming of his mother and the Hunter's knife, though in his dreams it was his father who held the blade. He woke with a terrible thirst. The eye where the Hunter had slid the blade under the skin was throbbing and itched so badly that Jens pulled himself forward so that his face touched the ground, and the pressure of that was nearly as good as scratching it.

But it was not long before the itch became a burning pain and Jens could hardly see at all. He called out for help again and again, but no one came.

A few hours later, Karl returned to the docks, dragging the body of a black hound with him. He threw it close to Jens.

"That's what happens to the Hunter's enemies," he said, and left without another word.

It was not long before the rats were running over the

hound's body, so many that they nearly hid the dark color of the hide. The only reminder of the creature beneath was the shape the rats made.

Jens forgot about his own pain at the sight of the hound he had met in the forest before, the hound who was Liva's mother. Did Liva know her mother was here? Did Liva know her mother was dead? She must have come yet again to try to protect her daughter.

And what of Liva? Frantically Jens began to pull on the ropes that held him until his hands were so raw, they looked like bulging sausages. The only reason he could keep at it was that there was no feeling remaining in them, for the rope had been tied too well.

After half an hour of pain, Jens had one hand out, though it was badly torn and bruised. He was working on the second when he heard a voice behind him.

Jens turned and saw the Hunter's son, Dofin.

Jens looked around to see what other of the Hunter's men had come, but Dofin was alone and was missing two fingers on his left hand.

"Ah, you noticed this," said Dofin, holding up the three remaining fingers. He wiggled them. "A lesson from my father. To remind me who and what he truly is and how little I matter to him."

Jens did not know why it should make him sicker to think that the Hunter used his stone knife on his own son than on all the others he had already hurt with it, but it did.

Dofin held up a steel knife then and moved to Jens's back. In a moment his other hand was free, and he sagged forward. Jens was overcome with the sudden return of circulation to his hands. Then he got to his feet, ready to run.

But he hesitated at the sight of the hound's bones. He could not leave them behind, for Liva's sake.

"My father thinks he has cowed me. In fact he has given me more power," said Dofin.

"How can that be true?" asked Jens, distracted for a moment.

Dofin waved his mutilated hand. "This gives me more sympathy from those who hate my father secretly. And it makes it clear from first sight that I stand against him. There can be no fear that I am his spy. They will speak openly with me now, and I can begin planning against him."

"Why have you come to me, then?" Jens asked. "Do you think I can kill your father for you?"

"I came because you saved me once," said Dofin. "And because I see that I will need allies in places other than this town when I have defeated him."

Dofin held out the jeweled half circlet that the hound had given Jens, and which he had thought lost forever. Jens was speechless as it was dropped into his hand. "Thank you," he stammered out at last. He put the half circlet back in his pouch.

"When my father discovers that you are gone, as well

as the two from the jail, he will be very angry," Dofin continued with a smirk. "Anger makes him vulnerable. He does not see it, but it is so. He will bring out his dogs and spend time and energy chasing after you. And while he is gone, I will be working against him."

So Liva and the boy from the jail had already escaped from the town. Jens did not have to think about how to rescue them. He could find them in the forest and protect them from the Hunter.

"I brought you this, as well. To make sure you are not easy for him to recapture." Dofin handed him a bag.

Jens glanced inside. It held dried fruit and nuts, a curved hunting knife, some coin, and a fresh loaf of bread that had to have been baked this very day.

"I must go," said Jens. His focus was on Liva now. He threw the sack over his shoulder.

"You have a little time," said Dofin. "My father sent all his men to chase after a great white snowbird that no one else can see. He says it has great magic, but I think his hatred for magic has made him unstable at last."

"You cannot see the snowbird?" asked Jens.

"What do you mean?" Dofin's eyes narrowed. "Of course I cannot see it. It is not real."

Jens shrugged.

"You have seen it?"

"In the forest," said Jens.

"But how can that be? He says that it has great aur-magic, but he has no aur-magic, nor do you. So you should not see it at all, and I should."

"Perhaps it knows how to disguise itself when it wishes to go unseen," said Jens.

"But I would not hurt it," said Dofin.

"Perhaps not. But you are not all humans," said Jens. And he wondered whether Dofin might try to think of ways to use the snowbird for his own purposes, if he could, to stop his father. The snowbird was not a creature that would wish to be used.

But for now, Jens had responsibility to Liva—and the body of the hound. He looked around for a sack to carry the hound in.

"Is that so important to you?" asked Dofin, staring at the remains in confusion.

"Yes," said Jens.

"Will it help you fight my father?" Again, Dofin showed that he thought of his own battle before the aur-magic itself.

"It does not have aur-magic left in it, does it?" asked Jens. He could not tell for himself.

Dofin's eyes went wide. Then he seemed to concentrate for a moment, and shrugged. "No aur-magic."

"Then I cannot see what use it will be against him."

"But you want it still?" asked Dofin.

"I cannot leave without it," said Jens.

With a shrug Dofin took off his shirt and handed it to Jens, rebuttoning his jacket over his bare chest. Jens tied the ends of the sleeves together and made a kind of sling out of it.

Gently he moved the bones of the hound into the

shirt and then cinched the shirt together with the string around the neck. He lifted it to see how it would fare, and everything seemed to hold together.

"Now, hurry and leave this place, for your own sake and for mine. There will soon be a battle here for power over the city, and I intend to be the one who wins it," said Dofin.

"I wish you luck," said Jens.

CHAPTER TWENTY-TWO

Liva

LIVA WAS RELIEVED that the Hunter had chased after the snowbird, leaving her and Tern as if they no longer mattered.

Now they were nearly at the top of the hill above the town, for she had zigzagged to elude any traps. They went slowly for that reason, but also because Tern could not move swiftly and Liva was hardly any faster, after the draining touch of the Hunter's huge stone. She was no longer numb on her left side, but she could change only a little more than one arm now, an arm and a shoulder, no more. She told herself it was an improvement and she should be happy for it, but it was difficult.

She and Tern rested behind a great pine tree, one side of its needles gone yellow with disease or human pollution. They sat there in the darkness, as the termites and other insects rose up from the ground and marched around them toward the tree. It was being eaten away.

189

Liva put her hand out and let the termites march up her arm, then down her back. It tickled, but the sensation of other lives tied to hers was enough to make her think of her mother. In the rush of escaping from the Hunter and the excitement of seeing the snowbird once more, she had hardly thought of the hound's death. Now the loss struck her fully. It was like swallowing a stone whole, for it sat heavily in her stomach, and it made her feel that she could not move without feeling pain. She went over and over her last sight of her mother still living. Her mother's last leap, her last breath, her last sound.

She did not know how long she spent like this, but she had grown cold by the time she felt Tern's touch on her shoulder, and she looked at him long enough to realize that her head hurt and her cheeks stung from the salt of the tears and her rubbing.

Tern beckoned her toward something, and Liva had to come closer to him to see it.

It was a crab, white-shelled with black specks, smaller than Liva's hand. Liva bent down and stared at it, surprised to see it so far from the ocean. She had never been a crab before. She had never been any creature from the ocean. There were things she had left to do with the aurmagic.

It was a comforting thought.

She let Tern rest then, and tried to rest herself. She had not slept since she had entered the town two days before, and it was already turning cool in the dusk. Liva had no fear of moving at night, and thought it might be an advantage against the Hunter.

It began to rain. She could not sleep except in bits and pieces.

She thought it was a dream when she saw the white wings of the snowbird approach again in the dim light of the dawn.

The snowbird swooped closer, and then its wings enfolded her, healing her completely where the stone had cut her. The snowbird let off aur-magic as simply as it breathed, and all around it benefited.

Liva thought of Tern and hoped fervently that he was feeling the magic too, even if he could not take it all in.

The snowbird sang out. "Destroy." It might have been a threatening word, but the snowbird sang it with such beauty that Liva could only listen as the long, deep, drawn-out notes poured toward her.

Then the snowbird snatched her up in its beak and flew her into the air. It happened so suddenly and with such speed that Liva's head whirled, and she had to close her eyes for a few moments before she could orient herself. She opened them to see Tamberg-on-the-Coast below her.

The snowbird was circling around the edges of the port town, but Liva didn't know why. It had not spoken—or sung—to her since that first word, which might have meant almost anything.

Destroy what?

Destroy the town?

Destroy the Hunter?

The snowbird was very careful to hold her gently, but Liva thought that riding on its back would have been more pleasant. Perhaps someday she could fly with the feel of feathers beneath her fingers.

Then they were descending again, and the world seemed to blur around Liva. She could see nothing but streaks of color and had to hold her breath.

The snowbird let go of her before it touched the ground.

Liva screamed in terror, and then felt the ground a moment later. She had fallen perhaps her own height, no more than that. She found her feet and then took in her surroundings, feeling suddenly weakened. The snowbird tucked in its wings and nudged Liva forward.

They were in the street where she'd been left by the old woman in the cart. The street where her mother had died, fighting the Hunter. The street where the stone had stolen her magic. And the stone was right in front of her.

No wonder she felt so weak.

The street was nearly empty, for it seemed that no one wished to go where the Hunter might reappear with his men at any moment.

The snowbird was moving toward the stone but did not touch it. Instead it sang out "stone" to Liva. There was so much expressed in the tone of the music. Fear and disgust, wrongness, evil, and a future that was empty and without magic.

"Yes, I know," said Liva. "It's a terrible thing." Could the snowbird destroy it simply with aur-magic? But the snowbird pressed Liva toward the stone.

"No, please," said Liva.

"Carry," sang the snowbird.

"But my magic," said Liva. "It will hurt me." She was only just beginning to recover. The snowbird had so much more magic than she did. Surely it made more sense for the snowbird to take the stone in its claws.

But if the snowbird were to pick up the stone without any protection, how much of its magic would be numbed and taken away? Far more than hers, for it had more to give.

And how could she refuse anything the snowbird asked?

"Destroy stone," sang the snowbird.

Liva bent down and lifted the stone with all her strength. She inched it closer to her chest and then forced herself to wrap her arms more tightly around it. It took all her will not to thrust it away. The feeling as her aur-magic went numb again was like freezing slowly, being filled with ice from her breath to her bones.

Then the snowbird picked her up in its beak once more. She felt a moment's pinch, and she was flying. With a few flaps of its wings the snowbird was gliding over the currents above the ocean. Liva could hardly see a hint of the town on the shore, but ahead was an island. A tiny island, hardly more than a mound, really. The snowbird headed steadily for it. As they drew closer, Liva could see that there was a hill on the island topped with an enormous stone of the same whitish gray as the one in her hand.

The snowbird jiggled her a little, and Liva was afraid that she'd be dropped with the stone onto the island.

"Destroy stone, destroy stone," the snowbird sang, with more urgency.

At last Liva understood. She must drop the stone. From this height, the thinly layered stone would shatter and be destroyed. Liva wished she could shatter all the stone on the island as well, but she could not see how to do it. Which meant that the Hunter would always have a place to come back to, to get more stones and more blades for his knife.

This stone, however, would be gone. Liva had to feel satisfaction at that.

She counted to three, then let it go.

She watched as the stone fell, growing smaller and smaller. She listened to the sound of the impact of stone on stone, and saw the tiny cloud of dust that rose from the island and then was gone.

There was little immediate relief in the release of the stone, though Liva's arms and chest ached afterward with the strain of lifting the stone's weight so long. Worse than that, as the snowbird flew back to the shore, Liva could still not feel her own aur-magic. The wind rushing into her face and the sound of the ocean distracted her from all else.

But as the snowbird flew, its magic slowly suffused her. The snowbird left her near the tree where Tern still slept. It called out a song, one with no word that Liva could find to match in her own mind. Something about promises and magic and the shining of the sun.

"Home," it said.

"Yes," Liva promised it. "We'll go home." Home to the cave. Her home, and now perhaps it would be Tern's as well. If they could get there without the Hunter stopping them.

The snowbird stepped back, preparing to fly away.

Liva thought of asking it to take her and Tern all the way back home, but she had tried to speak in the language of snowbirds herself before and could not. With the loss to her aur-magic now, she was sure she could not. And perhaps the snowbird had more important matters to attend to, things to do with the aur-magic that she could not understand.

When the snowbird was gone, she woke the boy, and they set out into the forest.

As Liva walked, she realized anew that her mother would not be waiting for her. That the black hound would never nip at and scold her again. That the cave would be empty when she arrived in it, as it had never been empty before.

Liva gasped air in, then sobbed and sobbed. In her ears there was nothing but the sound of grief.

Chapter Twenty-three

Jens

FLEEING, JENS SAW the shape of the snowbird high overhead. He thought it might swoop down to see him, but it did not even seem to notice him. And why should it? He continued on his way to the forest, which he reached while it was still morning.

He sighed relief at the familiar place. The town's scent of so many humans together, and of the fear that seemed to grow like reeds along a river because of the Hunter— all were gone. Here was the scent of cool and green life, and of death, too, but not of terror and mistrust.

Then he heard dogs behind him. The Hunter's dogs! Jens could not think he was worth the Hunter's trouble. They must be after Liva, who still had aur-magic enough to threaten the Hunter. Jens ran ahead as fast as he could, ducking and circling obstacles. He must reach Liva before the Hunter did.

Hours later, Jens dragged himself forward, limping, with a hand to his side. He felt like his insides might fall out. As if in reward, he caught his first glimpse of Liva in a copse where the sun glinted on her in human form.

He called out to warn her.

But he was so exhausted that he lost his balance and went down, the shirt sling with the hound in it slipping to the side.

Liva came for him.

He lay on the ground, staring up at the branches above his head—until her face was over his, her hand under his chin.

Her face was streaked with dirt and sweat. Her hair was long and dark and wild with burrs and tangles. She wore scraps of a shift she must have gotten in the port town, decorated with holes and greenish stains.

His mouth opened and a croaking sound came out, as though she thought he could speak in the language of frogs.

She put a finger to his lips. "Hush, Jens," she said.

He obeyed her.

In a moment she was pressing the juice of spring grass into his mouth to quench his thirst.

"The Hunter is not far behind," he got out in strangled bursts. "He has his dogs chasing us."

"I know," she said. "I have heard them now and again. I can feel them as well, with my aur-magic. I have that much of it left."

"So, the Hunter used his knife on you?" said Jens.

"He began, but he did not finish. My mother stopped him," Liva said.

"Hunter," whispered the boy next to her, and he began to tremble.

She turned to him. "Tern, don't worry. I will protect you."

"You two go ahead of me," said Jens. "Find shelter and hide yourselves deep in the forest. I will slow them down and distract them for as long as I can." The young boy with Liva was so young and fragile, Jens could see why she had brought him so far, though it endangered her life. He was what the Hunter meant to eradicate, in his search to cleanse the earth of aur-magic. Jens would do whatever he could to help her in this.

But Liva would not listen to him. "I won't leave you here. You've got to come with us."

Jens closed his eyes, exhausted, and shook his head.

"If you don't get up, the Hunter will catch me all the sooner," she whispered in his ear. "For if you are here, I will be, too. He will catch us all together."

And Jens knew she was speaking the truth. She never lied. It was part of the way of life in the forest she had grown up with. She had never learned deceit as other humans did. If she said that she would not leave without him, she meant it.

"Listen, Jens," she said urgently. "If he is coming to me, I want to face him on my own terms, in the land I know well. Let him come to me there, and see what he discovers about the true aur-magic—and the world around it. He only knows the tehr-magic of the port, of the people who have given up the forest. But my kin are there. And so is my magic." She pointed to the forest in the north.

"Ready?" she asked, after a moment.

He got up.

Tern hovered nearby, overburdened by the shirt sling that he had taken up, which held the remains of the hound.

Liva did not know what was in it, Jens thought. He would tell her when he had a moment. And then he would give her the half circlet. She surely deserved it now. She had proven that she was the protector of the aur-magic, and she deserved the symbol of the authority her mother had left behind for her. As soon as he had a moment to explain—that was all he was waiting for.

Jens carried the sling when he could, then sometimes allowed Tern to do it. The boy was eager to do his part, though he did not speak and did not look Jens in the eye. He sometimes mumbled to himself and sometimes sang songs, lullabies as if to a baby, but to himself. Jens recognized some of them as songs he had heard other mothers in the village sing. They had always made him feel a pang of jealousy, because his mother had never been able to sing them to him.

But Tern had had a mother and lost her, too. Jens felt that they had a connection. For both of them the songs were a reminder of loss, not an expression of privilege.

Through the singing, Liva pressed them both onward. She seemed to know Jens better than he knew himself. She stopped when he would have taken a few more steps, and she forced him on when he wanted to give up and lie down. But he never collapsed.

Jens still heard the belling of the Hunter's dogs echoing behind them, though sometimes they seemed to grow more distant. The dogs had to cross the river more than once to follow them, and Liva knew this terrain.

At night they stopped to rest, but Jens jerked awake what seemed like only moments after drifting off. There was a dog before him.

He thought it must be one of the Hunter's dogs, here already.

He threw himself between it and Liva. The dog leaped over him, and he fell onto the forest floor, knocking his mouth on a nasty stone.

But he turned back to see that it was not a dog at all, for its ears were too pointed and its body too thin to be a creature raised in a town by humans who fed it to keep it going strong. It was a wolf.

Liva was speaking to the wolf intently, with yelps and barks that Jens could only marvel at. The wolf gave one last word and leaped away.

"What is it?" asked Jens. "What did it say to you?"

"I told him of the Hunter and his threat to the forest, to the aur-magic, and to me. The wolf agreed to face the

Hunter's dogs in my place. The pack will go with him."

"How many?" asked Jens.

"Not enough," said Liva. She took a deep breath and held it.

"We must keep going," said Jens, trying to get to his feet.

"Yes," said Liva.

He tottered and she stabilized him. Then she bent down to give Tern a hand. He looked as bad as Jens felt. His face was dirty and bleeding; his shoulders sagged, and his cheeks, and his eyes.

But then Liva put a hand on Tern's shoulder, and the gray pallor of his face pinked and his mouth curled into a smile.

Aur-magic, Jens realized. She could give the boy a little, but not Jens. He had to keep going on his own.

At last, sometime between dusk and dark—Jens did not know anymore—they reached a large cave. Liva's home. The floor was swept clean, and there were wool blankets inside, as well as what might once have been a red velvet gown—to go with the red jewel in the half circlet, perhaps—now old and worn and wrapped into a ball like a pillow. Tern fell asleep next to it.

Jens wearily sat with his back against the wall while Liva went outside again. She returned later with some cold, wet leaves, to press to his aching muscles. He winced, then murmured his thanks. The pain became a little duller, and he slept drowsily until he heard her cry out.

He knew immediately what had happened.

She had opened the shirt-sling just outside the cave.

For once, Jens could do something for her that no one else could. He got up and stepped quietly out of the cave, placing a gentle hand on her back. Then he crouched beside her as she sobbed, giving her comfort.

When she could speak again, it was in a hoarse whisper. "My mother," she said.

"I brought her from the Hunter. For you."

Liva looked at him as if he were some miracle that had never been seen before, love shining in her eyes. "She fought him and I knew she had died. But I never thought to see her again."

"He treated her body as a prize, but when I had a chance, I knew you would want me to return her to you. I know there is no aur-magic left in her—"

"No," said Liva, shaking her head. "No, I did not expect that."

"But she belongs here. With you."

Liva opened her mouth, but she could not speak.

Jens opened the pouch and took out the half circlet.

Her eyes widened. "What is that?"

"It is from your mother," he said. "She showed me where it was hidden when she came to me this spring. I was afraid that I had lost it, but it came back to me, and now I know it is meant for you to have."

"I am no princess, no queen," said Liva. "My mother and father lived in a castle, ruled a kingdom. They had fine clothes and horses and servants. But I am only a girl in the forest."

"You have servants," said Jens. He pointed to himself and then to Tern. "And all of the forest serves you. All of the animals are yours to command. Think of that wolf and his pack. They went where you told them to go, never questioning your judgment."

"But—"

"You know the aur-magic as no one else does. You have sacrificed for it. I am not saying you have to leave the forest to wear this. But your mother meant for you to have it. She believed that you would grow into it. That you would become for those with aur-magic what she and your father once were, though in a different form. You can call yourself a mentor or a teacher, a guide if you wish. You may never step into another human-built dwelling. But that does not change who you are," said Jens.

Liva ran a finger along the gold line, around the ruby and then back along the gold to the end.

"Try it on," Jens urged her.

"Another day, perhaps," she said. "When I have finished with the Hunter. Then it will be mine." She handed it back to Jens and gestured to the hound's remains. "For now, I must bury her here, near my father."

Standing, she went to a section of ground that was soft and mounded, just outside the cave. She began to dig at it with her bare hands, throwing it out between her legs. Jens moved to her side and dug at the dirt with her, thinking he had never seen her look so regal as now, when she was covered with dirt and dripping sweat with fatigue. She glistened and she glowed with the richness of her kingdom, which was the forest.

Chapter Twenty-four
Liva

WHILE SHE DUG, Liva could hear the sounds of baying in the distance, and she knew the moment that each of the wolves died. She discarded the idea of calling more animals and sending them to fight the Hunter and his men. If Jens was right and the animals were her servants, she had no right to use them up so freely.

It was not animals who had created the Hunter and his stone knife. It was not animals who had given up their aur-magic to live in towns and away from the life and death of the forest. It was humans—her own kind—and she had aur-magic of her own to fight with, given to her for this very purpose: to save humans, even if it was from themselves.

At last, she finished pressing the dirt on the top of her mother's grave. In the distance Liva could hear the Hunter's dogs as they approached the cave. From the different barks, she estimated there were a total of twenty, from three different breeds: Ancient King, True Teeth, and Giant. Liva tried to use her magic to alter their course, but their human handlers were too vicious and had trained them too well. The dogs were slaves.

"I have this," said Jens, taking out a curved knife from his sack. "How many do you think you can kill with your aur-magic before they reach us?"

"None," said Liva stubbornly. The Hunter's dogs had been stripped of their aur-magic, but that did not mean she was free to kill them. The same was true of humans. She was responsible for them all.

Jens stared at her. "Then I will go meet them first and kill as many as I can before they come to you."

"No," said Liva.

"Why not?" he asked, his face hard and turned toward the forest.

"I'd rather calm the dogs, to offer the forest and freedom. And even offer the Hunter's men the same." She would save the Hunter himself, if she could, though she did not say this aloud to Jens.

"What?" Jens asked in astonishment.

"Stand at my side," she said. "That is all I ask of you."

"I am not afraid to die for you," said Jens. He stared out at the open forest, the cave at his back.

And Liva was not afraid to die for the aur-magic, so long as it lived on after her. That was the true cost of her parents' inheritance. They had been preparing her for this all her life, and she only just now felt the weight of it, far more than the weight of the gold in the circlet itself.

"You could leave this to me," said Liva. "Take care of yourself. Go far from here. I would be happy to know you were safe."

"I cannot do that, you know," said Jens. "If you are gone, there is no life for me."

"But—," said Liva. She could not look him in the eyes for more than a moment. Like coals, they burned her.

"If you want to keep me safe, keep yourself safe," said Jens. "Because I won't go on without you."

Liva felt a bursting sense of joy, and at the same time, a terrible, crushing fear. This was what it was like to be in love.

She had met him for the first time so young, but a part of her had known even then that he was her destiny. She had been working her way back to him since that day, and there had only been chance crossings. Now they were together again, and even the threat of the Hunter seemed nothing compared to that. They belonged to each other, as her mother and father had, through all of time, no matter what happened.

She put a hand out to him, and he snatched it to his face. Then he pulled her closer and she could feel his breath on her face. It was the wrong moment, and the right moment at the same time.

Liva pulled away painfully, her heart thumping in

her chest as if it belonged to Jens and wanted to leap to him.

"I must fight for the aur-magic," she said.

"I will fight for what you fight for," said Jens. "And for no other reason than that you wish me to. I know the aur-magic is part of you, and I will fight for it as I would fight for your eyes or your ears or the breath that fills your lungs."

Liva felt her eyes well up. She took a deep breath to regain control. "I think you know more about magic than you think," she said.

"Even a blind man can feel a fire," said Jens. "When it is burning so close to him that his eyebrows are singed and his teeth ache from the heat."

"I will do all I can," said Liva. "To make sure life goes on for as many as possible."

Jens turned back to her, his joy fading. "You mean the Hunter, too, don't you?" he asked.

Liva opened her mouth to answer, then shook her head. She did not want to argue with Jens about this. She should not have said anything at all.

"Leave him alive to come back at you? Surely you know better than that. You've lived in the forest too long. You never leave a wounded animal to follow your trail. It's dangerous. They can fight with new fervor if they have time to build up their anger. And humans are worse than most."

Liva knew he was right, and she knew that all animals

had the right to protect themselves if their lives were threatened. But she had never killed a human before. That was what the Hunter had done, killing humans to kill the aur-magic, and she did not want to become like him in any way. That would be letting him win, even if he was dead. He had said that aur-magic made humans animals, but he was wrong. The aur-magic made the world whole, animals more animal, and humans more human, and all of them more together than they were apart.

"Well, if you insist you will not kill them with your magic, why not use it in some other way?" said Jens, his eyes flashing with desperation. "You could turn them all into animals. Or fish, flopping around on the forest floor, unable to breathe air instead of water."

Liva shook her head. The aur-magic was not meant to be used that way. Humans should not be forced into animal form. And the animals in the forest did not deserve to have violent, angry humans forced among them, either.

"Then you could make it so that they all speak a different animal language and they run around in circles, attacking each other because they misunderstand each other so badly." Jens was gesticulating wildly with his hands. Liva could sense the tension in him. She thought he wanted to hold her as much as she wanted to hold him. Just feel each other safe and live in that moment.

But it could not be. "I cannot do those things, either. That is not what the aur-magic is. Or not what it should be, at its best. And I want it best."

Jens turned away from her, his shoulders hunched. "You must think me a fool. I say I am here to save you, but how can I help you? Without any magic, I am a man without a limb, a cripple you must feel no more than pity for, because you can do nothing for me, and must still watch my pitiful fumblings about."

Liva could see the beat of his pulse in the base of his neck, a line of vessel there that ran straight to his heart, and it throbbed. "I do not see you that way, Jens," she said.

He made a sound that was something between a laugh and a cough. "How could you not? You are a princess. A queen. And I am nothing. A boy from a village, who was turned out even from there. From the first time we met, you have seen only my worst, all my mistakes and weaknesses. Even my own father hated me." He stopped himself with a sudden hand lifted to his mouth.

"I never saw your father," said Liva steadily.

He tried to say she had, but Liva held up a hand. She had not meant it literally.

"I think I never saw anyone in your village except for you. Is that not the way it is during the day? The stars are still in the sky, but who sees them when the sun is so bright?"

"You cannot think of me as the sun," said Jens, snorting softly.

But she did. "With or without magic, you are the best human I know."

Jens reached for her. He held both of her hands with his own, and then he leaned forward. His lips met hers, and then Liva did forget about everything else. The forest, the magic, the Hunter, the end of the world.

There was only Jens and her and the air they shared and the feeling of two hearts beating together.

It did not last long enough.

They were still caught up in their embrace when the hounds, the Hunter, and his men crashed through the trees. Jens stepped away from her and watched as she put out a hand and one by one, each of the hounds lowered its head, whined, and walked away. Jens stood at her side and Liva thought of how often her parents, now buried next to each other, must have done the same.

"A fine trick, for animals," said the Hunter with a snarl. He took out his stone knife, flipping it over and over in his hands.

Liva forced her gaze away from the knife. She would not let herself be afraid of it. She knew what she had to do. "You don't have to follow him," she said, looking at the men who flanked the Hunter, one by one.

Their gazes slid past her.

"You think you will turn them away from me?" asked the Hunter. "They have seen aur-magic, and they know how terrible it is. You should not have gotten away from me in the first place. But I will take care of that now."

"You say they know how terrible the aur-magic is. Do they really?" Liva divided her magic into eleven different sprays, one for each of the men. It was something she had never done before, and she did not know how well she would do it, or whether she could continue for long. She used all the knowledge that her parents had given to her. She held nothing back.

The aur-magic flowed out of her in cold and hot, with bits of history attached. The stories her father had told— they were in this. Liva saw the first man who had merged into a wolf. She saw a woman who had given birth to twin sons, one a calf and one a boy. She felt the love of a woman for the man she waited for, but he never returned, because he did not know the way back from his magical change into a falcon. And she saw her mother and her father. She sent out her magic in waves.

The Hunter's men jerked and bobbed as they felt the pulse. They moaned and wept and cheered and danced.

She was winning! Liva was certain that these men could not stand against her now.

Then the Hunter took out his stone knife and flung it at her.

Liva saw it flying through the air.

She had one moment to decide whether she would try to evade it, and in doing so, give up the Hunter's men. It was what he must have intended, surely.

But she didn't do it.

She let the stone blade cut her in the chest, and for a moment she felt the aur-magic come out of her even more swiftly than before.

But then the aur-magic was absorbed by the knife. Liva gasped and felt the pain of the wound.

She was blind and deaf and dumb.

She reached out as if to the aur-magic, and she fell to the dirt in front of the cave.

She could feel a roaring in her ears as if she were falling quickly and wind was whirling all around her, but she did not land. The pain went on and grew worse.

The only sound that came from her throat was the soft sound of a human whisper. "Please," she said. "Please."

The Hunter's men stood, a few of them with dazed expressions on their faces, the others staring at her with wonder or horror.

She could give them no more. She had to hope that what she had done was enough.

But the Hunter did not seem daunted in the least.

He came toward her and ripped the stone knife out of her chest. He held it out as if to cut her again, perhaps the tiny cuts that he had used with Tern, to keep him alive, but dead to magic.

That was when Jens flew at him.

Chapter Twenty-five

Jens

*J*ENS WAS NOT afraid of the stone knife. He slammed into the Hunter and felt the knife slide away from him to the ground. The Hunter tried to reach it, but Jens kicked it away. Then he punched the Hunter in the face. It gave him great pleasure to see the Hunter's arrogant smile crumple as one tooth flew out and his cheek began to bruise.

The Hunter stepped back. "Help me!" he called to his men.

But his men were still confused from what Liva had given to them. Jens did not know what, but she had done something to slow them down. He did not care now.

He circled the Hunter, defying him to move closer to Liva.

The Hunter tried to fight him with words. "Do you think she cares about you? You, who have no magic of any kind?"

Jens grunted, then threw his fist into the Hunter's stomach.

The Hunter bent over double but pulled himself up and continued with his only weapon. "Well, perhaps she does. She is used to caring for small things. Animals and insects and birds. She sees the beauty in those things that are not truly human. And of course you are drawn to her, like a bear is drawn to honey."

Jens knocked out another tooth.

The Hunter's face dripped blood.

Now Jens could see that the Hunter was not as strong as he had first appeared. His arms and legs were muscled, but there was a softness to his torso, his stomach especially. He was used to easy living. In Tamberg-on-the-Coast he had his food brought to him. His men did what he asked. It had been some time since he had truly fought another with his own hands.

Jens did not expect to be given anything. This was his advantage.

The Hunter fumbled for the knife. "But what will you do afterward? If she wins and you remain at her side? Think, now. What will you do when all those around her have magic? When she goes to save those in danger, will you simply wait here in the cave for her? Killing food that does not hear you? Will you try to go with her and become a liability, another creature she must save?"

Jens swung at the Hunter, but this time the Hunter ducked and before Jens could recover his balance, the

Hunter had regained the knife and cut at Jens's side. Jens hissed in pain, and inched away.

The Hunter waved at him to get to his feet, and even then, holding back, said, "Catch your breath. I would never attack a man who wasn't ready for me."

Jens was not fooled by the lie. This time he didn't miss.

He struck at the Hunter's eye and felt the cheekbone break beneath his blow.

The Hunter cried out in pain, and his perpetual smile turned into a grimace. "You will regret that," he promised Jens. He gave Jens a series of kicks that left him retching on the leaf-strewn ground. Then he held out something under Jens's nose.

A stone as big as two fists.

But it was not meant for Jens.

"I never leave winning to chance," said the Hunter. "If one way is blocked, there is always another." He moved toward Liva, who was holding on to a tree for support as the blood—and more—oozed from the wound on her chest.

Jens saw her go white around the lips, but then she looked at him and tried to put a brave face on.

With staggering effort, Jens got to his feet. He had never had to push through so much pain before. There was no ignoring it. There was only agreeing with his body that it was too much, and then remembering his old movements, focusing on this one, and that one.

He had reached the Hunter's back when he heard a call overhead.

Jens looked up.

There was the snowbird, its great wingspan blocking out the sun.

The Hunter's men had been stunned up until now. But they gaped at the snowbird, revealed to them at last, and then began to run away.

"There it is! You see it now!" said the Hunter in triumph.

But the snowbird's flying was off-kilter, and it took a moment before Jens realized why. The snowbird was carrying something in its claws: a stone a thousand times as large as the one the Hunter had just used to threaten Liva.

What it must have cost the snowbird to carry it, Jens could only guess. But the creature had waited until now to use up all its strength.

"Watch out!" cried Liva weakly.

And the huge stone began to fall from the sky, crashing through trees as it approached.

Jens dived out of the way and just in time, for the stone shook the world when it fell and stirred up a dust that seemed to cover miles. When it had cleared, Jens could see that a great piece of the stone had remained unbroken, though other bits had turned to dust.

Jens stared at the snowbird, waiting for it to do more.

The snowbird did not fly away. Instead it landed near the stone. Jens could see that the snowbird was burned all along its underside, where its claws were. Where it must have held the stone as it flew. It could only have done something like this once, and this was the time for it.

The Hunter took out his stone knife and approached the snowbird.

"No!" shouted Liva. "Jens, stop him!" She staggered forward but could not get any closer to the stone.

Only Jens could.

He threw himself onto the stone between the Hunter and the snowbird, and only then did the snowbird come close enough to spread its wings over him. Protected from the stone by Jens, it was able to do its work. Jens could see the stone smoking as it was burned—he assumed by the snowbird's aur-magic. The smell was horrible, and there was a hissing sound. Jens could feel the stone melting like slag all around him. But he was untouched by all magic.

The snowbird sagged and fell on Jens's leg.

"No," gasped Liva, crawling forward. "The snowbird can't die." She was still bleeding from her wound.

"But it has already," cried the Hunter, gloating. "I've beaten it and the aur-magic at last!"

Jens pulled his leg from under the snowbird and moved to help its tottering figure off the stone. He looked back for one moment and saw that the stone had his shape imprinted into it. It was clearly not the same as it had been

218

before, and its new color showed this more than anything else. The stone was no longer white, but pure black.

The snowbird gave out a strange and beautiful cry as it saw the stone's destruction.

And the Hunter began to tremble. "No!" he exclaimed.

Jens began to feel something as well. It was a wonderful experience, like flying above the forest and seeing each creature below him, from the tiniest insect to the great moose. Not only could he see them, but he could feel them. He could know them and speak to them and feel as if he were a part of them.

It was the aur-magic, streaming out of the snowbird. Now that the stone had been destroyed, the aur-magic of the snowbird was everywhere—and unbelievably, thrillingly, Jens could feel it like a mist of heat. He luxuriated in it.

He thought that his aur-magic had been completely destroyed by the Hunter's knife at his birth. But with this much magic, he could feel a very small portion of it, despite his old wounds.

Even the Hunter could feel something, though it was no pleasure for him. He began to scream out in agony. He shook and then simply fell forward, dead, away from the snowbird and the stone.

The aur-magic had killed him. Jens thought he could not bear the glory of it. Whether it was his heart that stopped or something else, Jens did not know. But in the end he looked strangely at peace.

Jens stepped back from it all and felt as if he could not yet touch the ground. Was any of this real? Or was it part of a grand dream?

"You did it!" said Liva, smiling and putting one arm around his shoulder.

He picked her up in his arms and sat down with her a little bit away, caressing her hair. "But what did I do?" asked Jens. "I do not understand how I helped the snow-bird. I have no magic."

"Your lack of magic shielded the snowbird from the stone, allowing it to conserve its strength and pour its magic out, destroying the stone."

Jens thought of the first moment the snowbird had seen him, in the forest those years ago. He thought of the way the snowbird had searched his face, as if looking for something.

Perhaps it had seen something that Jens had never known was inside of himself.

It had defeated the Hunter and the stone with their help, but now it was paying the price. The snowbird was losing its feathers. Like the stone, it had changed color. It was grayish, and its eyes were dull.

It had given so much aur-magic. Could it survive that much loss?

Jens still felt warm with the aur-magic, but he had the feeling that it would soon dissipate. He had felt the aur-magic brush against him. That was enough for him.

Jens turned to Liva. She, too, looked gray and dull, though the bleeding from her chest had, at last, stopped. He had not realized how much she had suffered for this until now.

"Have you given up your magic, too? Like the snowbird?" he asked.

"Most of it," Liva admitted. "I think I have only as much left as anyone else now."

"I am so sorry," said Jens. "I know that the aur-magic was your whole life. I cannot imagine how it must feel to be without it." As soon as he said it, he realized he did know. He had always known.

Liva took his hand in hers. "It feels right," she said. "That much aur-magic was never meant to belong to one person. It's gone back to where it belongs, to the forest, to be shared. And I have no regrets."

He took out the half circlet once more and offered it to her. This time she did not refuse it, but she did not put it on her head. She took it into the cave with her and left it there, hidden in the midst of the debris.

Jens tried to tell her that her loss of aur-magic made her even more worthy to wear it, but she would not listen to him. It seemed that she had inherited more than the half circlet from her mother. She had inherited stubbornness as well.

Chapter Twenty-six
Liva

THE HUNTER WAS dead.

The stone was destroyed.

The aur-magic was safe once more.

Liva had done all that she had hoped to do.

But still, Liva felt empty.

She had lost her parents. She had lost her place in the world, and so much of her aur-magic. She felt as though she were a stranger in her own forest, and a stranger to herself. And she hated the thought of the half circlet that Jens had given her from her mother. It seemed to say to her that she had still not done enough, that there was work for her yet to do in the future.

She could not bear to look at it and avoided the part of the cave it was in.

Over the next several weeks, Jens tended Liva's chest wound until it had begun to physically scar over. She found she did not speak to him except a word now and then. She knew she should have been kinder to him. It was not that she did not love him anymore. She did. But she did not know who she was, and she felt bursts of anger she could not control.

After a few weeks, Jens took Tern to his old village in hopes of finding someone there who had lost a child and would care for a child who had lost his parents. Liva hugged Tern good-bye and felt an ache at missing him, but she knew that she was too young to truly be a mother to him. Perhaps she would visit him, but for now he needed to move on and forget.

In midsummer Liva stood in the forest by the cave with Jens, and she did not know what to do. She felt as though she had been put back in the jail with Tern, only the walls were smaller, and with each breath that she took, they closed in farther and farther.

She told herself that it was not as though she had no aur-magic left at all. She had a little, though it was very small in comparison to what she had had before. And besides, this was the way that other humans lived all the time. She knew this was the way her parents had lived since her birth, and that Jens had felt this much aur-magic for only a few short moments. But her sense of the animals around her was so restricted. She could remember only a few words of any animal language, and she could not change her form at all. Not even one hand.

She could sense the animals within a stone's throw, but she could not see them from the inside. She saw the shape of them vaguely, like a cloud in the sky, and she was not even sure of that.

"Do you think the snowbird lived?" asked Jens. It had limped once, then surged to the sky. They had watched together as the snowbird had faded into the distance, but they had not seen it since then.

"I don't know," said Liva. "It carried the stone so far, and then gave up so much aur-magic. But perhaps it might go on with less, like I do."

"It is the last of its kind," said Jens. "And now the snowbird has done what it was meant to do. It would be easier for it to die. I don't know how such a creature would live like that, in a world so changed."

Liva wondered whether Jens was also speaking of her.

"Now that you are well again, I think we have things to talk about," said Jens.

"What things?" asked Liva suspiciously.

"You know, it is not the aur-magic that makes you who you are," said Jens quietly. "Or the half circlet, either."

Liva's head jerked up. "What do you know about it?" she asked, knowing she was rude.

Jens did not take offense. "You can talk to me about anything," he said. "I hope you know that."

"I don't want to talk about it," said Liva. It would only bring back all the things that she could never have again.

"I never said you had to talk to me now," said Jens. "It can be in a week, a month, a year, or at the end of your life, when you are dying. I will be there for you, whatever you need."

Liva took a breath and held it. Jens, with her, for the rest of her life. She hadn't thought of it that way before. "I do not know—" She didn't want to hurt his feelings. She loved him still, but she just felt too small for that love now. As if it could burn her up if she wasn't careful. She needed time to find herself again before she could give herself to him.

"I thought I would stay close by," said Jens. "In the treetops, as I did before. I could come to see you now and again, when you wished it. I would not come without your invitation."

"Oh," said Liva. She slowly unfurled the fists that she had made and tried to unknot the other places in her body that were tense with trying to hold the last bit of magic she had left. "That will be fine."

"Good." Jens kissed her on the top of her nose, just a light brush of his lips.

Liva looked at his lips for a long moment after he pulled away from her, but she did not press herself to him.

Jens whispered, "I could see you in the eyes of a fel-frass and a pika, and in the eyes of any animal form you took. I saw the kindness in you and the determination."

"I was kind because the magic showed me the heart of all living things," said Liva. "And I was determined because my whole life, I have known that my purpose was magical."

"Listen," said Jens. "Do you think I am nothing because I have no magic?"

Liva was silent.

"Do you look at me and see all that I do not have?" he asked. There was real anger in his voice, and Liva could see the jump of the vein at the base of his throat.

"You know I don't," said Liva.

"Then why do you think I would do that to you?"

"I—"

"Why would you do it to yourself?"

Now both fell silent.

Jens stared at the stone that still held his imprint. "I felt the aur-magic," he said, his voice rough. "Through the snowbird. Don't think I have no idea of what it means. You had years more than I did with the magic. Can't it be enough?"

Liva thought of her mother then, with her lame leg. She had never complained about it. It limited her movements frequently and caused her pain always. But it was simply a part of life for her. She had accepted it and gone on.

Why couldn't Liva do the same?

There was the river.

And the oak tree with the broken limb.

The craggy rocks that stood like a sentinel on the mountains above.

What else did she need? She had her home, if only she could be herself in it.

Chapter Twenty-seven

Jens

A YEAR PASSED. LIVA and Jens lived apart, lives intersecting sometimes for an hour, sometimes for a whole day. Liva found herself drawn more and more often to the village nearby, to answer questions about the aur-magic. Or children and their parents sought her out, for advice, for stories, and for reassurance that the aur-magic was as it was meant to be.

Still, Liva did not wear the half circlet. But she was growing into the role she had been meant for. Jens could see it. He did not press himself on her. He simply waited for her to see what she wanted, and he hoped he would be part of it.

One night Liva saw the bite marks on his side after Jens encountered a hungry boar, just managing to evade it.

"If I had my old aur-magic back," Liva said absently,

"I could heal them in a moment, without a scar, with hardly a memory of it."

"I'll keep my memories, thank you," said Jens. "They are all that I am." It was what she had said to him, once.

Liva looked up at him, and Jens was sure she was thinking the same thing he was, because her lips reached for his. She had not kissed him at all the first several months. But now it happened more often, almost every day.

He could taste the life in her, sweet and strong.

"Sometimes I don't know if what we have is enough."

"Enough for what?" asked Jens.

"My parents had a love that lasted a thousand years," she said.

"We will have to concentrate ours then," said Jens. "Into a hundred."

That summer he secretly went about making a house in the treetops, in the dense part of the woods south of the cave where he had once lived alone. He found wood that would go just right together or cut it with his knife so that the notches dovetailed together. He used rope from the village to pull it up and put it together. Three rooms: one for her, one for him, and one for both of them together.

He was afraid that Liva would want to stay in the cave, but to him the place was too full of the Hunter's attack and the loss of her aur-magic. And her parents' deaths.

In the fall he brought her to the base of the tree and

tilted her head up so that she could see the sun sparkling down around the tightly drawn wood.

"You like it?"

"I love it," said Liva fervently. "As I love you."

He liked that look in her eyes.

That night, as they arranged bedding in the two separate rooms, Liva said, "What about the wedding?"

"Wedding?" echoed Jens stiffly.

"We could go to the village. Or to Tamberg-on-the-Coast." She smiled at Jens.

He felt as though his skin had burst open with bright love he had been trying to keep inside.

"Oh?" he said casually, though he knew she could see the smile on his face—so wide, he thought it might leave him aching at the stress on long-unused muscles.

"I am curious about the way it is now. I did not think much of it before."

"I have heard of changes," said Jens.

"What kind of changes?" asked Liva.

"The Hunter's son has taken power. I think he calls himself Duke now, instead of Dofin."

"Ah. He sends messages to you?"

"Of a sort," said Jens, not wishing to brag about his own importance. He was not lord of the forest or anything of the sort. But he understood it now, and he made sure that the village kept to its place while the animals kept to theirs. "He is very keen on keeping me away from the town, however. And you. He fears your reputation

229

with aur-magic will subsume his own."

"Do you think he will be better than his father?" asked Liva.

"He could hardly be worse," said Jens. "Besides, he has a little magic, and I think he has felt enough cruelty in his life to try to avoid it now. I hope."

"So that leaves the village." Liva nodded. "Your father is no longer there, you know. He has gone south, in search of his fortune."

"Has he?" said Jens.

"Tern is there," said Liva. "He is our only family, in a way, though he prefers to remain there. And we had our first conversation in the village, did we not? It seems right to go back, after a fashion."

"If you are sure," said Jens shyly.

"I am sure," said Liva, and she kissed him until he believed that she was.

Jens went to the village alone and found that in the time since the Hunter's death, there were many from Tamberg-on-the-Coast who had come to villages in the forest beyond it, no longer so afraid of the aur-magic and the animals.

One of these was a priest who wore a tattoo above his left eye to mark him as one who loved the aur-magic. Jens told Liva about him the next day, and Liva tracked his movements until there was a chance to ask him for a private ceremony in the forest.

On the day they had chosen, Jens surprised Liva by

climbing out of the tree wearing a white jacket and trousers he had traded several skins for. They were a little small for him, and the stiff shirt itched at his throat, but when he saw the look in her eyes, he forgot all that.

She wore a gown of deep blue with gold stitching up the bodice and shimmering, white-gold sleeves. Jens had seen her at work on it, though she always hid it when she caught the first glimpse of his head appearing in their tree house. She had traded skins to the women in the village and had somehow gotten the fabric for this.

"My mother told me once that her wedding day was the only day she had ever been truly frightened," said Liva, smiling.

"Of your father?" asked Jens.

"Of herself," said Liva, "and of the life she saw ahead of her, shining as a diamond in the light." She took out the half circlet and put it on her head proudly. It fit her well.

"Perfection is a hard ideal," said Jens, and he trembled in awe at the sight of the woman who was to be his wife.

But she smiled at him, and he knew that he was her match in all the ways that mattered.

Soon the moment came when the priest asked Jens if he had a ring. Jens produced one made of wood and polished to a sheen. The wood was from their own tree, and Tern had put a little aur-magic into it.

Now Jens could see her stiffen and take in a gasping breath as she felt the ring on her finger with her other hand.

"Is anything wrong?" asked the priest.

"No," said Liva softly, eyes alight.

"And do you have a ring for him?"

Liva took out one that had been made from black stone. Was it possible?

Jens stared at the ring as Liva put it on his finger. He thought he could feel something in it, like an echo of what he had felt when the snowbird had channeled the aur-magic through him.

"How?" asked Jens.

"If I told you all my secrets before we are married, what would we have to talk about afterward?" she asked.

The priest pronounced them husband and wife and said they might now kiss and love each other "with abandon."

Jens did not need any more encouragement. They kissed there in front of the priest, and then climbed together to the tree house and kissed again. Together, they made it their home.